Border Crossings

The sloop *Gonçalo Velho* (renamed *Yug*) in the 1940s.

Border Crossings

Manuel Tiago
(Álvaro Cunhal)

Translated and with a foreword by
Eric A. Gordon

INTERNATIONAL PUBLISHERS
New York

First English language edition, 2021 by International Publishers Co., Inc. / NY
by special arrangement with Editorial Avante!

Translated from the Portuguese by Eric A. Gordon © 2020
Foreword by Eric A. Gordon © 2020

Library of Congress Cataloging-in-Publication Data

Names: Tiago, Manuel, author. | Gordon, Eric A., 1945– translator, writer
  of foreword.
Title: Border crossings / Manuel Tiago (Álvaro Cunhal) ; translated and
  with a foreword by Eric A. Gordon.
Other titles: Fronteiras. English
Description: First English language edition. | New York : International
  Publishers, 2021. | Summary: "A collection of fictional accounts of the
  crossing national boundaries"— Provided by publisher.
Identifiers: LCCN 2021033022 (print) | LCCN 2021033023 (ebook) | ISBN
  9780717808731 (paperback) | ISBN 9780717808809 (epub)
Subjects: LCSH: Tiago, Manuel—Translations into English. | LCGFT: Short
  stories.
Classification: LCC PQ9282.I23 F7613 2021 (print) | LCC PQ9282.I23
  (ebook) | DDC 869.3/42—dc23
LC record available at https://lccn.loc.gov/2021033022
LC ebook record available at https://lccn.loc.gov/2021033023

ISBN-10: 0-7178-0873-4   ISBN-13: 978-0-7178-0873-1
Typeset by Amnet Systems, Chennai, India

This book is dedicated
to the treasured memory of
Juan José Guerrero Ibarra (alias Rubén Parga),
the late husband of Eric Gordon
who crossed many borders in life.
He was blind,
so as Eric completed each of these stories
he would read it to him by telephone
in his Mexican exile.

Table of Contents

Also available from International Publishers
in its series of fictional works by
Manuel Tiago

Five Days, Five Nights
"devoid of the stilted political speechifying sometimes
found in political fiction, the novella manages to capture the
complexities, loneliness, and bravery of ordinary people"
(*Monthly Review*)

The Six-Pointed Star
"a breathtaking novel of heartbreaking vignettes"
(*Culture Matters*)

The 3rd Floor
and Other Stories of the Portuguese Resistance
"exciting and suspenseful…I could not put the book down
as I read the four stories, each in one sitting.
Each of them is a page-turner."
(*People's World*)

Foreword

By Eric A. Gordon

ARE you ready for a whirlwind *tour du monde*—a world tour? Well, at least a European tour. By sea, by land, and by air.

A lucky 13 stories are gathered here, and in them Manuel Tiago rises to his most lyrical in his descriptions of nature and landscape and to his most humorous as he regales his readers with tales of amusing contretemps, mixed signals, false identities, linguistic mistakes, and narrow, fortuitous escapes.

The first entry in our Manuel Tiago series, the novella *Five Days, Five Nights*, could easily have fit into this book. It's the tale of a young comrade forced to leave Portugal and pass over an unmarked border to Spain, guided by an older, crude and somewhat sadistic man. It turns into a poignant coming of age story.

At the risk of dating not the work but the translation, I had the pleasure of rendering these episodes into English during the year 2020, when much of the world was hiding in hibernation to keep the COVID-19 virus at bay. At a time when travel, both foreign and domestic, was dicey at best, and for all practical purposes out of the question, it gave me great satisfaction to do some space travel as well as time travel by immersing myself in the many different worlds Tiago summons up in these stories.

In these fictional accounts of crossing borders, the reader will visit foreign cities, see brilliant visions and landscapes, sail the oceans, scale mountains, board ocean liners, trains and planes, communicate in a number of foreign languages, and engage in a kind of political tourism, meeting helpful comrades all along the way. There are also, of course, the discomforts of travel—close quarters, nasty bugs, exhaustion and bloodied feet, dangerous encounters, spies, police, rough seas and cold.

The author had no doubt heard all these stories, and many like them, over half a century of fighting fascism, finally setting them out in truthful, if not literal form, as he explains in the following note. Some stories don't seem to have much specificity as to their time frame, while others are explicitly late 1930s, before World War II broke out, or late 1940s, after the war.

It's often remarked that to understand the truth of any particular era, a time and place, it pays to read the great writers of the time. One could start with Homer, perhaps, but certainly Balzac, Tolstoy, F. Scott Fitzgerald, Austen, Machado de Assis, and many others. I might hesitate to place Manuel Tiago in those elevated ranks, but he has left us a body of vivid documents of what the world looked like, to him and to people like him, in those years of struggle for democracy in his homeland.

One theme that pops up in story after story here is that of communication, cooperation and collaboration. No one makes these journeys alone. They are aided by a global support system that recognized the critical importance of these crossings. Comrades traveled to the socialist countries to gain knowledge and expertise, both ideological and technological, using false identity papers that had been meticulously prepared by master forgers in the service of a socialist future.

United in spirit, it is heartwarming to see the ways people give freely of themselves to assist the traveler, offering wisdom, safety and comfort to the greatest degree possible.

At the same time, when the journey comes to a successful conclusion, there's a matter-of-fact, get-on-with-it attitude that doesn't allow time for complaints about what happened or didn't happen along the way.

When he contacted his liaison in Madrid, the comrade asked if the crossing had been tiring.

"It was good," Gabriel answered.

The comrade did not understand his meaning. Or maybe he did. He didn't press the point; there were urgent matters to attend to.

Information was shared strictly on a need-to-know basis. It could be fatal to know too much.

One thing that is noticeable in this thematically unified collection is a larger space than in much of Tiago's other writing for women to show some agency and character.

"The Hold" is very likely autobiographical, at least in part. Other stories in this collection may be as well. *Álvaro Cunhal— Fotobiografia*,[1] a large-scale photographic treatment of the author's life, briefly discusses a trip taken in 1947 in these words (my translation): "With the objective of reestablishing relations with the international Communist movement, he goes to the Soviet Union, via Yugoslavia, with the help of the Communist Party of that country, with whom he conducts conversations. On his return trip he has talks with representatives of the Communist Party of Czechoslovakia, the Communist Party of France and the Communist Party of Spain. During this trip he related the intense activity of the PCP which, since the end of the Thirties until almost the end of the Forties, was conducted in complete isolation in a Europe subjected to war and in large part occupied by fascist armies."

A brief technical observation: In Tiago's book, remarks made by others in Russian, German, Spanish, Italian, French, are rendered in the original language, and the Portuguese translation is footnoted. The use of these languages was clearly playful and exotic on the author's part, but I felt that the fluidity of conversation was awkwardly interrupted by this solution. I have modified the translation in those passages to indicate enough of the language being spoken and, where needed, provided a simultaneous translation, but all integrated, successfully, I hope, into the text proper.

Once again, I wish to thankfully acknowledge those who read the manuscript and offered their helpful suggestions: Bill Gregory, Francisco Melo, Gary Bono, Janice Rothstein, John Mueter, José Oliveira, and Steve Johnson.

---

1. Comissão das Comemorações do Centenário de Álvaro Cunhal, Lisbon: Editorial Avante!, 2013, p. 56.

BORDER Crossings is a collection of stories. Stories are fiction, and should be read as fiction.

The essence of the events narrated here and the thread in each story—of clandestine border crossing, along with the planning, the circumstances, the solutions, often with the direst of difficulties, indeed the greater part of the incidents related—correspond to the experiences of many men and women who lived them in real life. Some of these men and women are already dead, others still living.

However, because stories are literature, because writing stories is not recording history, because fiction is imagination, fantasy and dream, in each of these tales and in each of the characters there is a diversity, blended into a whole, of instances, situations, characteristics and experiences.

No one of these stories happened just so. But everything that is told, in every story recounted, happened. Everything in these stories is fiction and everything is reality.

So if the reader is led to believe that things happened just as they are narrated, you may be sure you are not mistaken with respect to historical truth.

September 1998

—Manuel Tiago

Border Crossings

A Good Crossing

1

VALENTIM'S store was situated by the side of the road. Though in an isolated location, it was a hub of community activity. The true center and point of reference for local life, as much for Old Town as for the settlement of Palhó, was Valentim and his store.

He was regarded as the most respected and esteemed man in the area, scrupulous in his dealings. Others strove to fulfill his expectations of them.

From time to time, as it happened that one summer morning, there was some unusual excitement at the store.

A car stopped at the door and two men entered. From behind the counter, a woman appeared.

"Ah, it's you, Sotelo!" And after casting a quick glance at the other new arrival, she added, "I'll go get him!"

She didn't take long. Tall and thin, with a cap on his head, Valentim shook hands with one, then the other, with the strong

grasp of a wiry, bony hand. He had them walk past the counter and led them inside the house.

"One or two more days. You can stay here," he said to Sotelo's companion. Apparently, he already knew what they were
there for.

2

Gabriel spent two days there. They were memorable, for the
hospitality, the tranquility and the sense of security. For how
carefully the crossing was planned. For the confidence among
the populace that the comrade enjoyed.

He would cross the frontier with friends who were carrying
coffee over to Spain.

"Contrabandists?"

"No, no, that wouldn't be the right word," Valentim corrected. It's a difficult life, he explained. Part of the year they
worked far away on country estates. The rest of the year, they
were unemployed. People in all border regions engaged in
smuggling. Without it they wouldn't survive. Yes, they dealt
in contraband, but they weren't contrabandists.

They dined and talked.

On the appointed day Gonçalo appeared, a short man of
few words.

"He's going to guide you to the other side," Valentim
explained. "He'll come for you later today."

3

Gonçalo showed up just after midnight. With an embrace from
Valentim and a kiss from his wife, the two departed.

After half an hour they met up with the others, obscure figures seated on the ground, with sacks of coffee at their feet.
Their faces could not be discerned, only the diffuse mass of the
group. When the two men arrived, they all stood up without a
word, took hold of their sacks and started on their way.

Slow and somber in the night, following an unmarked trail
that Gabriel couldn't see, they advanced in a silent file through

deserted fields. Once every hour or so, they put their bags down on the ground and sat a few moments to rest. Then they resumed the march.

While the company crawled along without a sound, the atmosphere was hardly silent. Awakened by the passage of humans, dogs never let up their barking. Their proximity was indicated by the faintness of distance or the vigorous sounds nearby. Some rough and terrifying, others sharp and irritated, they charted the travelers' path through the dark of night. It was a dangerous symphony that could reveal their route to the Border Guard, directing them where to find the hikers on the trail to intercept their crossing.

The people of Old Town and Palhó took wise precautions. They knew the terrain better than anyone. To throw the Guard off, they deviated from the route and, before returning to it, passed next to one farm after another. And the dogs there continued to bark, filling the immensity of the countryside and muddling the aural signposts of the itinerary.

The starry sky lent the night an even greater majesty, lights designed with painstaking variety and harmony, either in masses of a gentle glow or in the shining flare of brilliant sparks. Here, unlike other places where an angle of starry sky might peek out from behind a mountain skyline, the complete dome unfurled, huge, open and untouchable, anchored on the distant, circular horizon of the plain. Other than on such a plain or on the open sea, there is nothing that compares to this starry vault that invites an unhurried gaze until it fades out with morning.

The heavenly spectacle almost made Gabriel forget the gravity and risk in what they were attempting—to secretly cross the border. When they stopped to rest along the way, he stretched out for a moment with his back on the ground, contemplating the spacious sky and listening to the dogs, their howling dying away in the distance.

Turning over, he propped himself on his elbows to look about, still unable to distinguish his companions' features. He could only perceive the blur of silent bodies with their coffee sacks at their sides.

Showing remarkable understanding and discipline, they neither spoke nor smoked, for a gleam of light, even from the end of a cigarette, shines in the dark night like a star, and words, even spoken in a low voice, carry across distances in the silence of a still atmosphere.

He could not see their faces, but he knew and felt that those men were workers, his companions—some, perhaps, even his comrades. And, idealist that he was, one thing weighed on him as he took stock of this novel experience—that he couldn't get to know them, talk with them, share with them some moments of work and struggle in their lives.

4

It was still night, the group stopped to rest, and no one could see the faces of the people sitting on the ground with their bags. In a quiet voice, Gonçalo said, "We're in Spain already. We'll separate here. They will continue on their way, and we'll go on ours."

The two men rose and departed from the group. They followed some established paths until dawn, when they came upon a paved road.

"I'm returning to Old Town," said Gonçalo. "Up ahead is Rosal de la Frontera. It's a safe place. Ask where you get the bus to Seville. You won't have any problem."

And indeed there wasn't any. When he contacted his liaison in Madrid, the comrade asked if the crossing had been tiring.

"It was good," Gabriel answered.

The comrade did not understand his meaning. Or maybe he did. He didn't press the point; there were urgent matters to attend to.

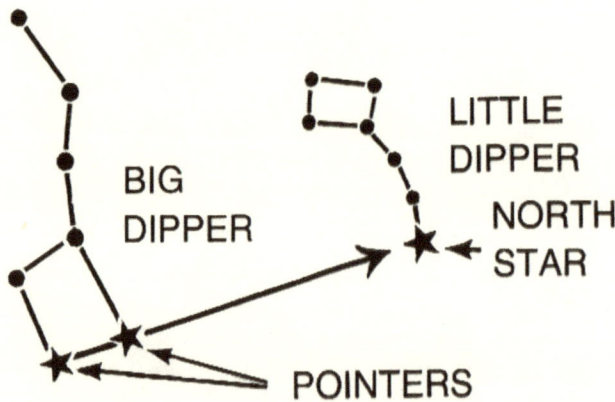

BIG
DIPPER

LITTLE
DIPPER

NORTH
STAR

POINTERS

Design by Pearson Scott Foresman (public domain)

Spain Lies to the East

1

THE news spread fast. Barra the river boatman had escaped from Caxias. And what an escape! Only possible by a careful, creative study of the situation, showing startling proof of his daring, his soberness, his self-control and composure.

For years on one of its prison floors, Barra watched the routines, the shifts, and how the prison guards and sentinels transitioned from one shift to the next. He observed the schedule of each new National Republican Guard contingent—the GNR—as it arrived at the fort replacing the one before. He noticed that frequently, at daybreak, before the changing of the guards, a few of them left in shirtsleeves, with a towel around their necks, and took exercise on the grounds in front of the façade, or just breathed in some fresh air.

He realized his plan to perfection the next day at the change of the GNR guard. He arose early, called the guard on duty and asked to go to the latrine located at the end of the corridor that ran from one end of the fort to the other. He followed unhurriedly and, when they got to the sizable atrium where the corridor passed by the entrance to the fort, and where sentinels were posted, seeing the guard turning his back, he got into line. He entered the atrium with slow steps, his towel around his neck, approached the doorway, stopped right in front of the sentinels' cabin, looking outward onto the grounds and the open air.

"Good morning," he said.

"Good morning," they answered.

He remained standing there a few more seconds and then, without looking back, left the building at a leisurely pace, crossed the grounds, and reached the trench. There, once again, he paused, performing exercises with his arms as he had seen some of the guards do in their usual morning routine.

On one of the prison floors, an inmate who had gotten up to look out the window, could hardly believe what he saw. "Whoa! It's Barra! It's him all right! What's he doing in that outfit? It can't be!"

There was no time for second thoughts. With his customary self-assurance, Barra disappeared over the trench, that is, outside the fort.

The guard who had accompanied him to the latrine mentioned to his colleague, just at that moment of changing the guard, that there was a prisoner at the end of the corridor in the latrine. The relief guard on duty waited and waited and, surprised at how long it was taking, went to see what was happening.

The alarm sounded: big commotion, running back and forth, armed guards on all sides, and Jeeps racing out of the prison. In vain. No one ever saw Barra again.

2

Comrades in the house that took him in made contact with the Party, and Alfredo showed up. Calm as Barra was, Alfredo was full of vitality. As soon as he walked in he embraced Barra, then did so again more strongly, and yet a third time.

"Hey, my friend, I can't believe it. We missed you. We're in rough times and there's so much to do."

If he was thinking up tasks for Barra, he was mistaken. The general perspective on his situation was quite different. They thought it dangerous for him to remain in the country. Best would be to get him over the border and have him stay there for a while. Now, under the Spanish Republican government, things were not so bad there.

"Whatever you think," Barra agreed, shrugging his shoulders.

The problem was crossing the border. On the left side of the Guadiana River they had seized people. The same had happened in Porto, and Lisbon had no contact with the north. The decision was made, but even after long consideration, no solution was found.

Every time Alfredo came, he got more desperate. Barra could not go on staying in these friends' house.

"Stay as long as you need to," said Rafael, the owner of the house, who had been Barra's workmate.

"Don't worry about us," his wife Josefa added. "We're here for you."

But when they observed suspicious people prowling on the street, they had to arrange another hiding place for him.

Then Alfredo made an unexpected proposition. "I'll take him there!"

"You? Impossible!" his comrades objected. With no support, they wouldn't find a safe route and the two of them would be caught.

"I'll take him," Alfredo insisted. Besides which, he had already taken other comrades close to the border, and had passed over with a professional border guide.

"Over where?" a comrade asked.

"Over there," Alfredo responded with a chuckle. "You just have to walk east."

"Ridiculous!" And they did not take his offer seriously.

That's where the matter would have ended, had any other solution come into view. As no one found any, and Barra's situation, as he was now hopping from one house to another, was getting more dangerous all the time and even unsustainable, they wound up assenting to such a crazy proposal.

"Finally!" Alfredo exclaimed, laughing. "Such a simple thing and what a pain it was convincing you."

3

Barra, with his mustache grown out and a hat as his disguise, and Alfredo in ordinary clothes, brazenly undisguised, took a train to Alentejo and from there a bus to the left bank of the Guadiana. Midafternoon they stopped in a small village Alfredo had chosen.

"It seems I passed through here the other time," he explained to Barra. "The border isn't far."

They ate at a tavern, then walked several kilometers on the road and later through open fields, their backs to the sun.

They walked for hours on a plain whose horizon, defined by oak trees and lower scrub oaks, seemed unchanging as they hiked the long distance. Night fell over a clear sky as the atmosphere cooled off.

They would have continued trying to walk in a straight line, always to the east, if they hadn't unexpectedly encountered an undulating terrain with slopes and hills that forced them to switch back in irregular directions. Alfredo began to hesitate. They proceeded in the dark, first in one direction, then in another, indecisively. Suddenly Alfredo halted and swore. "Dammit! This is bad," he admitted. "On land like this I don't know where Spain is any more."

It was time for Barra the river boatman, an expert on nights on the water, to interject his wisdom. "Look at the sky," he told his companion in a quiet, assured tone. "Up there... Do you see four stars in the shape of a square?"

"No. No, I don't see anything, there are so many—"

"You're not looking in the right place. Up there, up there...," and he pointed with his finger.

"Ah! Now I see it!"

"See? And now do you see there's a row of stars coming off it, like the tail of the square?"

"Wait...wait. Yes, I see it."

"Now imagine that the two stars on the end of the square are tied in a line, see? Now extend that line five times its length. Are you following me? What do you see?"

"What do I see? This is very complicated. I'm not seeing anything—"

"Look closely. Don't you see one bigger star shining bright?"

"Wait...yes, now I do!"

"That's the North Star. It points north. Turn toward it, like this, and open your arms... Your right arm is now pointing east."

"Toward Spain," Alfredo corrected him happily.

"Toward Spain," Barra repeated, in a lightly mocking tone.

"Good, we're right then, let's continue," Alfredo said.

They walked, on and on, with no more surprises, and decided to rest a while. They sat themselves against a tree trunk, and wound up stretching out and falling asleep.

Alfredo awoke in the half-light of dawn. He had no idea where they were nor how far from the border. He was annoyed with himself, and also unhappy because, having figured the route was much shorter, he had not brought anything to eat or drink. Patience: There was nothing else to do but move forward. He woke Barra, and they continued.

As day broke, the countryside changed, with little houses here and there glowing in the eastern sun, marked paths on the ground, and then—surprise!—a paved road. They ran across it and kept going in the direction of the sun emerging on the horizon. They found another road and a village a few hundred meters ahead.

"Let's go! We need to know where we are and how far we are from the border."

As they crossed paths with a man coming at them from the opposite direction, he greeted them. "*Buenos días!*" he said in passing.

"*Buenos días!*" Alfredo said in response. Finally, they were in Spain.

They walked farther on to another town near a bigger road. There they hailed a passenger bus headed for Seville, and took their leave of one another.

"So, in the end, very easy," Alfredo said with pride.

"Not so easy," Barra replied. "Safe return."

4

Venta de Baños was the name of that town. Alfredo had never heard of it, nor did he know how far it was from the frontier.

When he left for Spain, he felt driven by limitless energy and powerful self-confidence. Now he felt enervated by the effort accomplished and the anticipation of the equivalent effort ahead. On the first leg, he had enthusiasm for the task to be done and for the company. Now he'd be all alone that whole long march back through unfamiliar and deserted fields.

With more foresight than on the trip east, he found a road-house, ate until he felt satisfied, and stocked up on bread and cheese. The cheese wasn't the best, but that amazing Spanish bread was so tasty—double-milled flour, in eight sections, tender crust, and soft, compact core. All prepared for the return hike, he set out on his way.

It was midday by then, and he started out with the sun on his left.

He walked all day, hour after hour. He tried to keep to his westward direction, crossing roadways, avoiding settlements, following and at times straying from pathways. At twilight, exhausted as he was, his legs in pain and almost immovable, he sat against an oak tree, not able to go any farther.

He unwrapped his pack of bread and cheese with the idea of having a bite to eat, but in his fatigue, and almost unconsciously, he wrapped it up again.

He realized that he desperately needed to rest a while. But since he was in too open an area, he decided to find a better place to sleep for the night.

Catching sight of a small tree-topped hill at the end of the plain, he chose that for his sleeping spot. He'd certainly get there while it was still light.

It grew dark, however, sooner than he thought. Also, he had misjudged the terrain, for it was more uneven than it appeared. Night fell before he arrived at the hill.

As he trudged onward, he was barely conscious that he was now treading the path of a paved road, when a sharp beam of light struck him straight in his eyes for just the briefest of seconds. In a flash he was able to see, out of the darkness, the radiator and windshield of a small vehicle, and two standing figures. Then came a shout with an unmistakable Spanish accent: "Halt!"

He jumped off the road, heard a gunshot, then another, and he ran aimlessly across the field to get away from the danger.

He learned two things: That he was still in Spain and that he couldn't stop now. He had to overcome his exhaustion, his aching, obstinate legs, the growing heaviness of his eyelids, the desire to go not a step farther and allow himself to fall, close his eyes and stay put there without having to decide anything more.

He pressed on, marching all night long. Remembering Barra's lesson, he looked at the sky, found the North Star, concluded he was going the right way, toward the west, toward Portugal, always west, toward Portugal, no stopping, no stopping, evermore enfeebled and addle-headed.

He collapsed on the earth, like a heavy, limp sack. With eyes closed and a crushing will to sleep, nevertheless he couldn't. He sensed the total loss of his strength, a faintness, and a fear of never recovering from it. Anxiously attempting to stop feeling and thinking, after a tumble of confused imagery, a memory came back to him in exacting detail of another border jump he had been involved in and that ended badly.

5

As clearly as if it were today, the old comrade and the border guide leaving by the road in the dark, just as he had seen them that fateful day. By the road instead of going right into the fields as had been agreed. Leaving, going away, disappearing into the night. The comrades meeting the guide, a vagrant who wandered from market to market throughout Portugal and Spain, that rigid, expressionless face. Right away he didn't like him for some reason, who knows why. Maybe the way he talked or his manners. And serious, earnest Januário at the steering wheel, with him at his side, and the old comrade cowering in the back seat nodding off to sleep. Januário, serious and earnest, with his profile at the steering wheel, the car at night on the endless road, now the agreed-upon crossroads, a deserted locale and dark all around. Januário turned around in the opposite direction and stopped. No border guide, where was the guide, dammit. But now, there he was, a dark silhouette standing out from the light background of a whitewashed wall. And then the old comrade stepping out of the car, meeting the guide, and the two of them departing down the road, why down the road and not through the fields as had been agreed? Going away, retreating, disappearing into the night and he and Januário, in the parked car, waiting for something and not knowing what. Waiting, waiting, and suddenly a loud shot, the sound fading away gradually into space. And another isolated shot, this one barely heard in the distance, far, far away, ever farther away….

Lying in the cold damp earth, he woke up with a jolt, fully conscious of the situation he was in. It was a dream, but so precise, just as it had happened.

Now he recalled it all lucidly. Januário tore out, with the headlights off, cutting directly through the fields, without seeing what was in front of him, the car rocking and vaulting on the uneven ground until he stopped a few hundred meters in. After a while, coming from the border area along the road that the old comrade and guide had just taken, they saw a small car and immediately after a pickup truck rushing past at great speed and lighting up the street….

Sinking once again into a profound stupor, into a turbulent confusion of images, the guide and the old comrade, side by side, going away on the street, going away, disappearing into the night….

6

He came out of his torpor, his shivering body curled up in the humid earth. Now he could clearly assess the situation in which he found himself. He recognized the imperative need to get up, start walking again, and however he managed to do it, reach Portugal again.

He stood up and started walking—"walking" being dragging the burden of his legs, his panting breath, the fever paralyzing his body, making his head and his eyelids heavy as lead. But he could not stop. If he fell down again as he had fallen back there, for sure he would never get up again.

And without expecting it, what he saw brought him a blaze of happiness.

By the light of the sun's first rays, on a hill maybe half a kilo-meter away, in a compound of uniquely situated buildings, shone the unmistakable whitewashed walls of an Alentejo farm.

7

They found him sleeping in the hay. "Hey, friend, what hap-pened?" a man squatting next to him asked.

He opened his eyes, dazed. He mumbled something about having made a great trek, then fell asleep again.

This man certainly knew much of life. Perhaps it was not the first time he had harbored someone. Maybe he had even helped someone cross the border. He didn't ask anything more.

The man, his wife and son received him and took care of him. He got better. He washed up and shaved himself with a razor blade they lent him, and with which, for lack of experi-ence, he gave himself four gashes on his cheeks. The man and the son brought him to a village where he caught a bus that carried him to a railway station. Ticket, train, Lisbon.

Sílvia knew he had returned from a risky mission and immedi-ately took tender care of her companion. She heated the water for his bath, prepared his meal, helped him to eat and climb into bed.

He slept until the middle of the following afternoon, and when he awoke, Sílvia was by his side watching him. "How do you feel?" she asked sweetly, caressing his forehead.

Smiling and in good spirits, Alfredo pulled her into the sheets. They got up when it was already getting dark. He got dressed, left to use the public telephone, and returned. Two hours later a comrade appeared.

Alfredo gave a short report, relating that he had left Barra in Spain on a bus to Seville, and by now he'd surely be in Madrid. The return to Portugal had been slower than anticipated, but in time everything got resolved.

"Terrific!"—the only word the comrade came up with in response.

A few days later, at a meeting, someone who had originally disagreed with the plan insisted on giving his opinion.

"Just because something has been done," he commented, "doesn't make it wise."

"Would it have been wiser if we still had Barra here? Or if he had already been apprehended?" Alfredo replied.

The other didn't give up easily. "And if you two had been taken prisoner at the border? Wouldn't we all be held responsible?"

Alfredo returned home in deep thought. Maybe, yes, maybe it had been adventurous on his part, but as far as he was concerned, two things were certain: If it's necessary to take risks, you take risks, and if another similar case should arise, he would once again be ready to take that risk. Ruminating along those lines as he walked home, letting his imagination run on, he pictured himself at night in the fields looking at the starry sky and orienting himself as Barra had taught him.

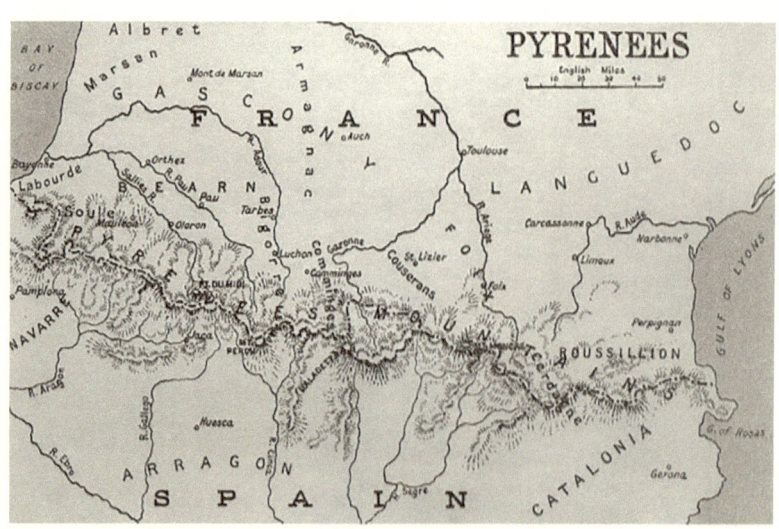

A map from Sabine Baring-Gould's 1907 *A Book of the Pyrenees* (public domain)

The Pass Through the Pyrenees

1

JUST after midday, Pepe and the two Portuguese men arrived in San Sebastián. A comrade waiting for them at the station exchanged a few words with Pepe and, in an old jitney, drove the group to a restaurant, where they ate. Pepe said his good-byes and left. The others left, too.

The jitney passed through streets flooded with sunlight and busy with the commotion of summer vacationers, and then turned onto small, quiet streets and a secondary road, gradually leaving suburbs and settlements behind. Night fell, and they stopped at a sloping path, keeping their silence.

Coming clandestinely from Portugal, Abel and Francisco sought to cross the frontier into France over the Pyrenees. As it had been so far, everything happened so quickly that they saw nothing of the city of San Sebastián, whose beauty everyone praised. Through the jitney windows they only caught a glimpse of the majestic outlines of the mountains through which they would pass. Pepe, who had accompanied them from Madrid, had told them, "You'll be going up to the top. The border line is right there."

An indiscreet disclosure, or a joke? It was hard to understand why you had to hike all the way to the mountain summit just to cross the border.

Such musings were interrupted by someone who approached cautiously and leaned against the jitney window, tapping on the glass with his knuckles. The driver got out and went to speak with him. Minutes later, with everyone gathered outside, the newcomer gave some instructions.

They could not bring any baggage with them other than the package of food that the jitney driver had brought for them. It was all they would have to eat for the two days of hiking.

They had to throw away their shoes and wear the canvas espadrilles that the newcomer handed them.

The crossing would be in three stages and at each stage they would be led by a different guide. This fellow would be the guide for the first stage, and he would leave them on their own at a determined location on the mountain, where the second guide would come for them. The same would happen with the third.

With all that explained, and everyone in their espadrilles, they took their leave of the comrade from San Sebastián, and the guide indicated for them to follow.

"I'll carry the package," said Abel.

"Never mind, I'll take it," Francisco said.

2

At a slowish pace, they passed over paths and terrain without marked boundaries, sometimes forested and other times uncovered and open to the sky. In the dark of night, the two friends never realized they had begun their mountain climb. They walked several hours with a long, lazy stride, as the guide showed them. Their bodies, enveloped in the still atmosphere, heated up with the hike, as the air gradually turned lighter and cooler. They were increasing their altitude without feeling any distinct incline.

At one moment, when they were traversing an even, grassy terrain, the guide stopped. "We have to drink a little fresh water." At that, he unexpectedly dropped to the ground with his face toward the soil. Surprised, they moved to help him, but he got up nimbly and drew his forearm across his mouth. "Drink, it's good."

Drink? How? The guide explained, and they lay down as the guide had and, placing their mouths on the thin thread of water running gently through the grass, they satisfied their thirst.

They got up, and then, still amazed, lay down again and drank some more.

They continued walking well into the night. Despite the pure atmosphere, they couldn't see stars in the sky. By now they could feel the incline on the hills, giving shape to the irregular mountains. Eventually they stood at a point where, in the shadows, they could make out big piles of leaves and branches.

It was then that Abel, forgetting the instruction he had received not to speak in a loud voice, let out a cry: "The food package!"

"Didn't you pick it up?" Francisco asked.

"You were the one carrying it."

"Dammit! We left it behind when we had our drink of water."

There was no consideration of going back. They didn't even say anything about it when the guide, who had stepped away for a moment, returned to tell them what they needed to do now.

Stretch out on the ground, and he would pile a load of leaves on top of them, leaving an opening they could breathe through. In the morning, the next guide would come. That's what they did, and he left.

The heavy weight of leaves and vegetation stayed in place and sheltered the two friends against the growing night cold. With their stomachs toward the ground on a slight incline, they crossed their arms under their chins, with only darkness surrounding them.

Suddenly, from afar, a light attracted their attention and revealed the position they were in. It was the headlights of a car that, far away below them, was driving along a road. The spectacle seemed so extraordinary that, forgetting the food package and the discomfort of their shelter, they stayed awake with eyes open through the blackness of space, until once again they saw the beam from another car, and then another, then many more, as if beckoning and greeting them from a distant mountain chasm.

3

Abel awakened first, hearing the sound of steps. He elbowed Francisco to wake up also. In the space before them the fog reached the ground. Then, almost in front of their faces, two feet girded in heavy boots appeared. And in short order, the vegetal cover was lifted and thrown to the side.

They got up with difficulty, exhausted from yesterday's hike and from a restive night. In front of them stood a serious new guide who looked at them sympathetically. *"Buenos días. Ready to walk?"*

Thus began the second stage, walking all day long with brief rest stops. At midday, the guide stopped in a welcoming location. He proposed it was time to eat and drink something. When he learned what had happened with the package of provisions, he made no response at first.

"Where one eats, two or three can eat." He said it so naturally, as he offered the little he had—bread, cheese, and a few swallows of wine from his canteen.

Restored, they took up the march until nightfall. They did not exactly understand the difference between the hike all the previous night and this one, in full daylight, where the guide was obviously worry-free. The guide explained. The previous night they had gone through greatly exposed areas subject to vigilance and patrols. Now they were passing through very high, deserted zones. Whoever knew these mountains knew how to choose safe trails.

A serious man of few words, the guide was nevertheless friendly and comradely; he made for good company and inspired confidence.

At day's end, as they rounded a mountain, a surprising landscape welcomed them. The space opened up to the east, and as far as the eye could see into the distance, there were the crests of the lacy mountains shining brilliantly in the sun, in contrast to the valleys and ravines below in black shadow.

The guide left them on that high point, in the ruins of a shelter whose existence in such a place seemed inexplicable. "Tomorrow's the last day," he told them. "They'll come for you early in the morning."

He said farewell, walked away a few steps, then returned without a word and left them the canteen.

4

The third guide did not appear early as they had been told. The two friends left the ruined shelter impatiently. Down below, the base of the mountains was still asleep in dark night, though the sun was already beaming its pure, clear light on the peaks. In this silent space, the cold, light air offered a refreshing invitation to breathe. Thus they spent hours, enchanted by the view, but freezing and overtaken with anxiety.

Finally, the guide showed up. He emerged from a much lower, distant hill, and approached casually, climbing the incline effortlessly, as the two men had walked their first day.

"*Bonjour*," he said in French, halting a few meters away. "Are you ready?"

They started walking the way he had come.

At one point, to their surprise, they looked west onto a grandly brilliant panorama. Standing out from the range of crags and mountains, a succession of descending slopes, lit up by the sun, revealed the brilliance of shining green pasturelands. Far below, extending to the north as far as one could see, lay a crazy patchwork of light and colors, fields, groves of trees and farmhouses attesting to the intensity of human life. To the west, also as far as the eye could take you, out to the long horizon line with the sky, sat the immense, shimmering stripe of the ocean.

In a short time they were walking over soft green pastures in a descent that left behind the rough, wild heights.

Yet another surprise awaited them. They heard low bell sounds, spaced out, short and melodious, coming from some

unknown place nearby. Finally they saw several cows peacefully at pasture, with no one around. Also surprising, here and
there, buckets full of milk, brimming with foamy white bub-
bles from having been filled not very long before.

Their reaction was quick and irresistible. Abel and Francisco
both ran and fell to their knees before those buckets. Placing
their faces to the lip of the steaming warm buckets, they drank
and drank and drank, and when they stood up, took deep,
satisfied breaths.

"How wonderful!" said Abel, forgetting that since he was a
boy, he never liked the taste of milk.

"Wonderful indeed!" Francisco agreed.

The guide watched them silently but watchfully. He made a
simple gesture to move along.

The descent completed, now with a hurried gait, quickly crossing roads and avoiding houses, they came to a city at the end
of the afternoon and were led to a pension. After introducing
them, the guide said goodbye and disappeared.

The hosts treated the comrades as though they were old
friends. They gave them clothes and shoes. They prepared hot
baths for them and served them a lovely dinner. After they
informed them that the next day a comrade would come and
get them, they led them to a room with two beds and wished
them a good night.

There was one unimportant detail they would never forget. When they took their baths, they felt bites behind their
ears and on their abdomens. And they saw a healthy colony
of ticks, some of them looking like minuscule crabs, others
round like little white berries. Surely they must have picked
them up during that night, covered with leaves, at the top of
the mountains.

"It's incredible we didn't notice anything," said Abel.

"I did feel something," Francisco replied, "but I thought it
was the leaves."

Arcachon oyster culture. Postcard, photo by Victor Faure (1900–1910) (public domain)

From Gascony to Portugal

1

COMMUNICATION from Lisbon confirmed the possibility for Luís to return. If he could clandestinely enter Spain and catch the Sud Expresso to Ciudad Rodrigo, a comrade could go meet him in Spanish territory and guide him across the border. Only two days' notice were required—by telephone, as they indicated.

In Paris, his French friends gave him an address: Jean Dupré, 14 Rue Maître Roland, Ville Neuve, Bordeaux.

He was a totally trustworthy comrade. His father, Émile Dupré, a Communist, had been shot to death by the Germans in a wave of imprisoned hostages in reprisal for an attempt against a Gestapo chief. Jean distinguished himself years later for having organized the secret return of Spanish comrades to their country. Maybe he could help with this case.

Train to Bordeaux, bus to Ville Neuve. The driver said there was a stop on the route just at the corner of that street. It was a short, quiet street of modest homes and yards in the outskirts.

Number 14 had a light wooden gate, a small, simple garden, and then the house.

A thin young woman with light hair opened the door. Yes, he had been expected.

"Monsieur Jean Dupré?" he asked.

The woman briefly said, "He's not here but he'll be coming." She called out, "Mother," and soon Luís found himself in a large room, seated before four women who regarded him curiously and sympathetically.

One had meticulously combed white hair, with a face of fine features and relaxed blue eyes. Two of them were in their thirties, the blond who opened the door, and the other, a brunette, both with different faces but similar in the way they expressed themselves. The fourth, in her fifties, was a little on the plump side. As soon as he sat down, she repeated what the blonde had said at the door, as though she were the first to say it: "He's not here but he'll be coming."

The conversation unfolded around the ordinary things of life—the questions everyone asks, and the responses everyone gives.

As if it, too, wanted to share in the reception, a black cat with emerald green eyes, which had settled into the young blonde woman's lap, eased itself slowly and heavily to the floor, came over to brush against the guest's legs and, after disappearing for a rotation around the house, returned, in one spry leap, to its berth in the lap from which he had come. For a few seconds, before he hid them behind his lazy eyelids, his emerald eyes lit up amidst the black blur of his velvety coat.

"That's Lord," the plump one explained.

Luís knew nothing about these women. Their talk could have been that of any other women. But just their talk. There was something else that was different—serious, austere, solemn, respectable—that he sensed from this unusual welcome by these four women facing him.

He was surprised when the black cat, jumping once more to the floor, snagged a panel of cloth that was covering the blonde woman's knees. On snatching the cloth, she exclaimed, "*Brutta bestia!* Naughty animal!"

"She's Italian," the plump woman said without further explication.

Later he would learn who these women were. The eldest, the martyr Émile's mother. The plump one, his widow. The dark-haired woman, her daughter, Jean's sister. The blonde, Jean's wife, who he now knew was Italian.

2

Jean arrived at nightfall. From Paris he had only gathered a mere idea of what this was all about. Now he understood concretely. The two young women and the aged grandmother left the room, and the remaining three discussed the situation.

"This won't be easy" was Jean's first comment.

He knew that before the Spanish Civil War and the Second World War, clandestine border crossings took place across the Pyrenees. After the war also, he, Jean, had organized many furtive expeditions for the Spanish comrades. But that came to an end. Grave events had led to their no longer using that system. The Spanish comrades had come up with some other solutions, but Jean didn't know what. Quite frankly, he didn't see the possibility.

"But we must try anyway," said his mother.

Jean didn't seem convinced. He reminded his mother of what had happened years before, after which, he refused to lend his assistance.

While Jean insisted on the difficulty, his mother insisted it was necessary to verify if it was possible or not. All right, Jean reluctantly agreed. He would study the question and see if something could be done.

The mother had a decidedly strong voice. Study what? Wait for what? In these things, life teaches that one cannot lose time. He could phone to Arcachon or Saint Martin-sur-Mer and make a quick trip there with Luís. It wasn't far, maybe the next day.

Jean wound up agreeing. He would try, but not the next day. He had other obligations he couldn't put off.

"Very well, day after tomorrow!" said his mother with a quirky smile.

So it was decided. They said good night and went to bed.

The room assigned to Luís was small and muggy. When he opened the window, a whiff of fresh air entered, along with the faint perfume of ripened fruit and an unexpected distant concert of croaking frogs—constant, sweet, and lulling.

3

Luís woke to a long day of rest in that tranquil house and the gardens that surrounded it.

The widow and her two children left for Bordeaux, where they worked. Remaining behind were the grandmother and the Italian.

Set before him was a lovely breakfast—*café au lait*, a nice crusty baguette, butter, cheese and a selection of homemade compotes. They left him to his own resources. If it appealed to him, he could go into the garden and pick and eat whatever fruit he chose, as if he were in his own home. And so he did.

The garden was tended to perfection. As they told him at breakfast, Jean worked hard at it every weekend, and the whole family worked alongside him. There were a vegetable plot, an orchard and a well with a shining metal cupola. Apple and peach trees, tomatoes, cabbage, lettuce, green beans climbing up stalks, everything seemed planned and measured, artfully arranged and designed.

He spent the morning walking around, happily picking and eating a peach with its velvet skin, and sitting comfortably in the sun.

The grandmother and Lucia, the Italian woman, prepared lunch, and he ate with them. Then they started talking. It was an unusually candid conversation.

Apropos the French and foreigners, the grandmother spoke of Lucia. It was a mistake to think the French don't like foreigners. Lucia was well loved by everyone. She had come from Auschwitz with Suzanne, Émile Dupré's daughter. Crawling out almost like a skeleton, she regained her strength in her friend's house. Nothing more would have been said if Luís hadn't asked why she didn't go back to Italy.

An uncomfortable silence followed in the wake of his question.

She doesn't like to remember all that, the grandmother explained.

But then, for some unknown reason, Lucia started to tell the story, all of it, her head bowed, her words slow and determined.

The village where she was born had been completely leveled by the Nazis. The population had been exterminated. Men, women and children had been led to a public square, forced into an enormous wooden warehouse surrounded by the SS with pointed guns. Gasoline, fire, everything in flames. And screaming, screaming, horrible screaming like you never heard. Only one woman escaped, and she hid in a pigsty. Old and demented when Lucia went there, she couldn't tell her anything about her family.

Lucia returned to be with her companion from Auschwitz. She married Jean, and now she was several months pregnant, as Luís could see.

4

After lunch, Luís took a little siesta and went out to the garden for another walk around.

This time he went farther from the house to the back of the garden, and saw a trench through which a smooth sheet of water was slowly running and giving off its green reflections. The trench divided the yard in two.

A rudimentary wooden bridge led to the other side, which was very different, with a few isolated trees, uncultivated shrubs and a couple of shacks.

He had just crossed the bridge when he heard someone calling, "Hey, hey!" He saw a thin old sunburned man sitting on the ground at the door of a shack, in a sleeveless shirt and a red cloth tied around his head.

"Hey! Come sit down," said the old man, pointing to the ground by his feet. Luís sat where he was told. The man didn't ask who he was, nor where he came from, nor what he was doing in the yard. He only asked, right away, "Tell me, do you like frogs?"

"Frogs?" Luís wondered.

Yes, frogs, the man confirmed. What's wrong? Was there anything in the world more delicious than frog legs?

Without continuing the conversation, he rose and quickly entered the shack, coming out holding a long pole with a strange metal rigging at the end. "Come, come!" and he took Luís to the trench.

In animated tones he explained what this was all about. Fixed at the end of the pole was a kind of harpoon. You set the spring on the harpoon and tie the spring to a strong cord. That's how he caught frogs. He looked for them on the surface of the trench. He'd choose the biggest one, point his harpoon, pull the cord, and *zap!* the spring released and the harpoon nailed the frog.

At that hour, in the midday heat, it wasn't the best time for the frogs to come out and pose quietly in the sun. But another time, he'd show him.

They went back to the shack. The old man entered to put away his harpoon, then came out and once more sat on the ground. He started telling his stories. One time, in a single afternoon, he caught forty frogs. Forty, can you believe it? Another time, he caught an enormous frog, a giant, such as he'd never seen before and never did again. "Like this!" and with his palms separated midair to show its size, he watched Luís closely for his reaction.

Finally he stopped talking, and signaled it was time for Luís to get up. He only said, "Come back whenever you like! It's been a pleasure to meet you!"

And he stood there rigid, watching his visitor retreat until he had disappeared from sight.

Back at the house, no one asked about his walk through the gardens, nor did he mention his encounter with the old man.

5

They started with Arcachon. Jean telephoned, asking the comrade to come to Bordeaux to the usual café. There the three met. Jean made the introductions: comrade Robert, comrade Luís, nothing more.

Tall and beefy, his white shirt hugging his torso, his face and arms suntanned, Robert attracted attention. He observed Luís with a restrained curiosity.

When Jean explained the objective for this meeting, Robert remained silent, shaking his head. He made the same response that Jean had made. "Not possible."

He elaborated: For a long time now, fishing boats out of Arcachon had not been going into Spanish waters. That's all he could say.

Jean did not give up. He spoke of internationalist solidarity and what it would mean for Luís to return to Portugal. Robert shouldn't say it's "impossible" without checking further to see if it was or not.

Robert didn't need to be begged. All right, he would see. Luís could come with him to Arcachon. Both of them would see. If he wanted, it could be right now. He had his car nearby and could take Luís with him. This was a good time, because many of the boats had returned and unloaded this morning. The fishermen would be in town the rest of the day.

Said and done. Robert drove Luís to Arcachon. They spent the whole afternoon on this question in the area around the fishermen's dock.

From bar to bar, café to café, on the wharf and on the street, they talked with one person after another. Robert knew everybody. He spoke frankly to all, and it was clear they treated him with respect. He spoke with everyone, but only with some did he call them aside, shared a glass with them and asked questions.

He didn't reveal the point of his questions. He only wanted to know for sure if any fishing boat continued to fish off the Spanish coast.

They all said no. Plain and simple, no exceptions. One fisherman, however, made a remark to which Robert had no response. He didn't understand why Robert was asking such a question. The whole world knew, Robert included, that for a long time, no one went fishing there.

At the end of the day, now having had a few too many, Robert walked Luís to catch a bus to Bordeaux.

Before he said goodbye, he drew close to Luís and told him almost in secret with a husky, low voice, there was one thing he didn't understand. "Truly, I don't understand." He was watching the whole time. Everyone was drinking, all except Luís. He was offering and paying every time, wasn't that so? Frankly, he didn't understand. Was Luís not feeling well? Was he sick? He didn't understand. "Truly," he didn't understand.

And, changing his tone, he added that he agreed with Jean. Jean had said to exhaust all possibilities and he was right. Jean was always right. He'd continue to look. But now Luís knew the way back. Come back whenever you want! They confirmed a date.

Returning to Bordeaux, Luís wandered through the city streets, and it was night already when he got back to the house.

He got off the bus at his street and followed the road in the dark. All of a sudden, something weird caught his attention. On the sidewalk were the shining eyes of some animal, and even more surprisingly, the animal crept silently alongside him, though at a distance. Only at the door did he understand what was going on. The animal suddenly made a break for the inside of the house, then, quite friendly, started rubbing against Luís's legs. It was Lord, the house cat.

6

They took the car to Saint Martin-sur-Mer. Jean was very familiar with his friends' habits. At lunchtime Jean and Luís entered a restaurant full of people, Jean asked the employees about Théodore, and they pointed out where, as usual, he could be found eating.

Jean chose a table for three in a corner of the room, told Luís to take a seat, and went over to Théodore, who looked visibly surprised, even displeased by his visitor.

As they ate a *choucroute*, they talked. Jean did not broach the subject right away. He asked about Théodore's friends, about his health, and how this one and that one were doing, and made a few comments about political events.

It looked like the conversation was not advancing any further when Théodore, who up until then had been eyeing the two visitors, interrupted him.

"No, Jean. No. You know very well, *c'est fini*. It's over." He had guessed the purpose of the visit.

Jean confirmed it, and as he started to delve into the matter, Théodore reacted excitedly.

"No. What happened in the past will not happen again. *C'est fini*." After a pause, "*…fini!*"

Then, speaking rapidly, but with his voice under control, he unleashed a chain of complaints, resentments and woes.

He never thought anyone would ever ask him for that kind of help again. Had Jean forgotten what happened? That he, Théodore, had warned them so many times of the great risks involved? Risks so big that one day, sooner or later, people would surely get caught? Had Jean also forgotten that the Party had not listened? Théodore kept on warning, yet they continued to do it. Exactly what he predicted wound up happening. When they disembarked on a deserted stretch of the coast, two Spanish comrades were taken prisoner and sentenced to heavy punishment. One of the Frenchmen managed to flee, got back on board and escaped. The other stayed there.

He was really taken aback that Jean should put a question like this before him because he knew perfectly well that Théodore's brother was in prison ten years now. "*Fini!*" This one was no longer to be counted on. Question settled once and for all. Théodore was a Gascon and that's how people in Gascony are.

Jean listened without interrupting. Then he spoke. About how the struggle was still going on against Franco, against Salazar, to achieve freedom, to set the prisoners free—and also to free Théodore's brother. He told him Luís wanted to get over the border, pass through Spain, then cross the Portuguese border to carry on the underground struggle in his country. "Forgive me," Jean said, but despite everything that happened, he had thought of him.

Théodore also did not interrupt. With Jean's first words, Théodore was still shaking his head no and making gestures of protest as if wanting to cut him off. Then he calmed down and got quiet and still. He could have been paying close attention to what Jean was saying—or maybe he was consumed by tragic memories.

Jean stopped talking finally. The three sat in silence. Théodore covered the check for lunch and without a word accompanied his friends out to the street. Only as he took his leave he spoke again, in slow, extremely calm tones. They should come back in two days. He'd think about it.

7

Returning to the house, Jean invited Luís to go with him after dinner to a meeting that night in Bordeaux. Luís objected that he was undocumented, and in case there were any incident, he didn't want to risk it.

Don't worry, Jean reassured him. He wouldn't be going alone, but with himself and other comrades, all solid people. No one would ask who Luís was. They were accustomed to seeing Jean with foreign comrades, and besides, Luís spoke French well. From his accent they would think, if anything, he was from some other region.

So agreed, they dined at home and that night went out to the street to await their ride.

Luís then noticed that, a few meters away, in the shadow, the old frog hunter was watching them. What was he doing there?

In time, a pickup truck with an open carriage stopped in front of the house. Jean signaled for Luís to climb on and, to great surprise, he similarly gestured to the old man and helped him to step over the truck's wooden sidewall.

Other friends were already on board, some standing, others stretched out. The three newcomers settled on the floor and the truck took off jerking along, the cool night air blowing on the company in strong currents from the fast movement.

They arrived at the grand pavilion at the market, full of people, flags, shouting and songs. Alongside Luís, the old frog hunter gave free rein to his enthusiasm. "What a Party, old man!" gushed the hunter. "There's not another one like it."

His enthusiasm glowed red-hot when the principal orator's voice, amplified by speakers not in use up to now, echoed so strongly that even the glass windows of the pavilion vibrated noisily.

"What a voice, *mon Dieu!* My God, what lungs!" the old man kept repeating.

One of the comrades in the group, seeing how Jean was helping the old man climb up and down the bleacher stairs, remarked, "He's so kindly toward his *grand-père*—"

"—his grandfather?" said Luís in shock.

"What? You didn't know?" the comrade asked, baffled. "The old man is the father of Émile Dupré, *héros national.*"

Back in his stuffy little room, Luís opened the window again. It was a little cooler now than the night before, the aroma of ripe fruit coming through on the caressing breeze.

In the distance he heard the incessant echo of frogs.

By now, surely, the old man must have reached his shack in the dark.

8

Robert was waiting for him in Arcachon on the Seafarers' Dock in the port zone, seated calmly at his usual table with a Pernod before him.

Luís asked the waiter for a beer, but Robert interrupted him. "Beer?" No, Luís was not going to drink beer, Robert wouldn't let him. He invited Luís to have some "Portuguese oysters," and with oysters you don't drink beer but a fine Bordeaux wine.

Why "Portuguese oysters?" In Paris, walking on the Rue du Faubourg Montmartre, Luís had seen hundreds of baskets of oysters with signs saying "Portuguese oysters" at the entrances to restaurants and bars, and he asked his comrades. He gathered different explanations.

"They come from Portugal, obviously!" one emigrant comrade confirmed. "It's one of the few things they import to France from our country."

No, a French comrade corrected. The oysters were in fact French, but they called these ones "Portuguese" because they were smaller.

They continued in that light vein, even adding a little suggestively that they were "Portuguese" because they were the most delicious.

Now in Arcachon, with two platters of shucked oysters on the table, lemon wedges ready to squeeze and a carafe of cold white wine at the ready, Robert revealed the mystery.

It was precisely there in the Bay of Arcachon where "Portuguese oysters" originated. Many years before, a fishing boat returning from the Portuguese coast with a load of oysters had shipwrecked here. The oysters found their true natural habitat at the bottom of the bay. Here they multiplied and formed a plentiful bed which never stopped producing.

They were the tastiest without a doubt. Above all so fresh and alive, with the squeezed lemon and the chilled wine on a hot day.

Robert arranged the dinner and offered it with proud satisfaction.

About the matter at hand, which they had set this meeting to discuss—the possibility of getting Luís over to Spain—not a word was uttered. Not even Luís brought it up, seeing it wasn't worth the trouble.

Like the first time, Robert walked with Luís to the bus stop. "Come back whenever you like," he said, as Luís seated himself on the bus next to a window.

When he got off the bus, the same scene repeated itself. On the dark sidewalk, joining alongside him, he saw Lord's shining eyes. And just as before, Lord walked with him up to the gate, where he rubbed himself vigorously against Luís's legs. They entered the house together.

9

The two men had hardly sat down in the restaurant when Théodore modestly and simply blurted out, "I will take you there myself." Without wasting any time, he laid out what needed to be done.

Luís had to confirm with Portugal, as he himself had said, the date they should expect him in Ciudad Rodrigo, and show up in shirtsleeves with no baggage. No one else would go with them in a little sailboat. Théodore would leave him at a spot on the Spanish coast near San Sebastián. Luís would disembark quickly and, following the route Théodore indicated, pick up the Southern train.

Théodore had studied the tides. Three days from now would be a good time. Once Luís had confirmed the date with Lisbon, he had only to phone from Bordeaux and show up.

It was all settled without a single word to spare and without further comment. The decisions and the actions spoke for themselves.

10

In those two days, the last with the Dupré family, they showed themselves as true friends and comrades in caring solidarity, reliable and honest in both conduct and feeling. In those last days they redoubled their attentions to Luís.

With eyeglasses screening her quiet blue eyes, the grandmother neatly sewed a vest with pockets that Luís could slip on underneath his shirt, in which he could carry his documents. Granny pursued the work with pleasure, stopping from time to time, removing her glasses and staring out without saying anything, her beautiful blue eyes fixed on the Portuguese comrade. Luís read in that look the consciousness and responsibility involved in what he was doing.

The widow, generally formal and businesslike, spent hours preparing a delicious specialty. She would not allow him to go away without trying it. She was cooking snails. She took them out of their shells, removed the tripe, made a mixture of butter, crushed ham and minced parsley, placed each snail one by one back in the empty shells, covered them well with the mixture, and put them in the oven with the opening of the shells face-up so as not to spill the butter when she removed them.

The delicacy was paired with a good wine. More than a delicacy, it was a keepsake to remember.

Lucia and Jean participated and helped with everything, though a disturbing incident with Suzanne upset the calm.

In the course of conversation about the weather, about the food, about the fruit, Suzanne got up to go into the city. Luís, who would never inquire about anything of a personal nature, asked a question which he immediately regretted—if Suzanne was going to meet up with her boyfriend.

The woman's face changed abruptly. She rose and with a bitter, almost aggressive voice, responded, "Never! Men are monsters." With that she impetuously left the room. None of the other family members offered any explanation. They continued as they had been. Embarrassed and remorseful, Luís neither apologized nor asked anything further. What had happened to Suzanne, always so affectionate, unpretentious and caring? Maybe in Auschwitz. Maybe things one simply cannot appropriately ask about, nor know or remember.

The Dupré family relations were so transparent, and at the same time everything was so individual, as much for each of them in particular as in their sum. Individual because everyone felt these things as one, as the inexplicable cause of the singularity, the presence and consequence of the war and the fascist terror and crimes that touched them all so profoundly.

What conflict, what problem, certainly of extreme gravity, would have led to such a situation not only with Suzanne but also with the old man?

Émile Dupré's mother, Communist, national hero, enjoyed the comfort of her family, house and garden, while the father was out there in back, on the other side of the trench, hunting down frogs.

People in the house knew that Luís had met the old man, concluding it naturally from his disappearances into the far yard. The old man knew that Luís was living there in the house, because that's the only place he could be. But not once did anyone, on one side or the other, make reference to it. The old man never said a thing about the family and the house. Nor did anyone in the house say even a word about the old man. With only one exception. One time, a little before lunchtime, Luís absented himself to go try some frog legs at the old man's invitation. Jean correctly guessed that's where Luís was going, discreetly pulling Luís aside, almost secretly, and handing him a wrapped bottle.

"Don't tell him it's from me."

These are the mysteries that no one explains and no one dares be explained. Such respectable enigmas in human relationships gain significance over time for being just what they are, great unknowns that command respect. That is when, in relationships between and among people, all is right and clear with safe and tranquil serenity.

The farewell, when Luís left, was simple. The old man said goodbye the night before, next to his shack. "I hope all goes well, my son."

The others gathered outside the door. One by one, the four women kissed the comrade. Jean drove him in his car to Saint Martin-sur-Mer. On the way, Luís could not concentrate on what he was about to do, nor what lay ahead—the passage through Spain to Portugal, the uncertainties and dangers that awaited him. He thought only of that family, feeling for them such immense tenderness and affection as though they were close, beloved relations.

11

Midmorning on the dock looked like any time of day. Two sailors, one with sunglasses and a hat with a wide brim to protect his eyes against the sun, the other bareheaded, boarded a small sailboat. After some brief preparations and raising the sail, they glided off smoothly straight out to sea.

Théodore sat at the stern with the rudder, adjusting the sail and steering the boat.

He chose an unusual course. Instead of hugging the coastline toward the south, he headed farther and farther west until land was out of sight. Then, in the following hours, he cut a wide arc to the southwest, then south and east until regaining sight of land, and then, at some distance, changing direction to the north. Anyone on land seeing the white sail would conclude—and this was the point—that the boat came not from the north and the French side, but from the south, from some other point on the Spanish coast.

They landed finally in a little inlet. Théodore gave Luís the signal to get up from the bottom of the boat and jump to the ground. Without losing time, Théodore made a quick maneuver with the sail, and headed out to sea again.

Just as Théodore had told him, Luís walked away from the coastline as though taking a leisurely stroll. There was the big shed poised prominently atop a white dune. And he found the faint pathway that gave out not far ahead. There he crossed the train tracks, and shortly after found houses, a street, cars, bicycles, everything that Théodore had mentioned.

He went to the station to purchase a ticket, wandered the busy streets of San Sebastián, and boarded the Southern train. He spent the entire night, now sleeping, now awake, in a third-class compartment full of passengers.

Still night, with a sports newspaper in hand, as instructed from Lisbon, he got off at Ciudad Rodrigo and left the station amongst a clutch of other people.

Outside, before he had walked even a few steps, a tall man approached him, wearing a beret and glasses with metal frames. Taking him lightly by the arm, he said simply, "Come with me!"

It seemed impossible: It was Custódio, whom Luís knew years before in the underground movement, and whom he had crossed paths with several times.

Casually, naturally, Custódio led him several streets away. "Everything okay?"

"Yes, everything okay."

They reached a plaza where they caught a taxi for Fuentes de Oñoro.

There, without a word, Custódio set off on their way. Leaving behind major streets, they walked along little byways into forested areas and empty pasturelands. It was still dark when they mounted a manmade hillock, on top of which ran a railway line.

All of a sudden, Luís stopped and grabbed his comrade's arm. Some ten or twenty meters ahead, in shadow but distinctly seen standing there, a border guard was facing them and certainly observing them.

Custódio showed neither haste nor anxiety. They crossed the rail line at a normal walking pace and saying nothing, the guard watching them the whole time. On the other side, they descended a gully, passed through some fields, and soon found themselves among houses and streets with a few isolated lights on.

They didn't walk far. On a deserted little road they came to a parked car. Custódio opened the door, told his friend to get in, then took the steering wheel and drove off.

"Done. You made it," was all he said.

Luís did not fully understand what had happened—above all, at the railway line with the border guard just standing and watching them go through. But he didn't ask. Besides which, he knew that if he did, Custódio wouldn't answer.

Photo: Heigeheige (Creative Commons)

Women Over the Soajo

1

THE two women left the country together. Together they had pursued a course of study. Together they returned. They got stuck at a certain point along the way. For reasons unknown, they did not receive the word to depart.

"So much to do down there, and we're sitting here, losing time," Berta lamented, tired of waiting.

"Losing time?" Manuela laughed. "What more do you want?"

There was nothing to complain about in either the hotel nor their comrades. The accommodations, the service, the meals—they had never known anything better. And such courteous treatment, the staff always asking if there weren't something else they'd like.

"I'm going to get fat here," said Manuela good-naturedly.

First thing in the morning, sausage and eggs, cheese and butter. As Berta could see, her clothes no longer fit properly.

"You know," Berta answered, "I miss our cup of coffee with fried fish left over from the night before."

During the day, they left the hotel without going too far, observing buildings and people, and visiting stores. After dinner, they went out again and, having once stopped at a bakery for cake and tea, they returned for the same every day thereafter. Manuela thought they must look like two single ladies living off their rental income.

In the hotel foyer, as they readied themselves for their walk, more than once they noticed another hotel guest sitting still and discreetly in a corner.

"Poor guy," Berta remarked, "always by himself and looking so sad."

And what if we invited him for a stroll with us?

They asked their friends at the hotel. No, there'd be no problem. It was a Brazilian comrade who also was waiting to continue his journey.

They extended the invitation, and he accepted with unexpected delight. The three went out for the usual promenade: a short walk, the bakery, cake and tea. They made light conversation, and the Brazilian was good company.

Returning to the hotel, they asked if he'd like to go out with them the next day too, and it was set. "Sleep well," Berta said goodnight.

They could imagine almost anything else, but not the comrade's response:

"Sleep?" Now? No, now he was going out, because only after midnight were the cabarets full of interesting things. Didn't they want to join him? Right now? Or the next day?

"I never would have guessed," Berta commented. "How reckless the comrade is."

Manuela found a certain humor in the situation. "Always sitting in the corner like that, his clever disguise totally fooled us."

They never had the chance to go out again with him. In the morning they received word that finally they'd be leaving the next day.

2

They ran into him on the next leg of their journey, in another country. They were having lunch in a restaurant when from the next table they heard the musical voice of someone asking, "*Un autre bifteck s'il vous plaît!*"—another steak, please.

It was the Brazilian comrade. They spoke at the restaurant exit and took a stroll around the streets. Once again they were together at the same hotel, a private, special hostelry like the other one.

The comrade was happy to meet them again, and now recounted much about himself. Like them, he was an underground party militant, from the Northeast, a region of misery and rebellion.

As they were expecting to be departing quite soon, they decided to meet again the next day.

"He's a doll, this guy!" Manuela gushed.

Berta smiled. "He sure is."

To their last meeting he brought a large package. They ate on the esplanade, and continued their conversation. He said how much he had enjoyed meeting them, two Portuguese Communists, and such lovely women. He wanted to leave them a remembrance, and it was in that package, something of value that people used in Brazil. He didn't wind up giving it to anyone in the country where they were, and now, given the circumstances of his return trip, he wasn't able to take it with him. So he would leave it with them as a keepsake.

Before they returned to the hotel, they shared an emotional farewell, because for sure they would never see him again.

In their room, they opened the package. To their shock, it was a typical, broad-brimmed hat from the Brazilian Northeast, an enormous hat!

How gracious a gift! But for them, too, impossible to take with them.

Before going to bed, Manuela stood in front of the mirror. "Did you hear what he said? 'Two lovely women.'"

"They all say the same thing," Berta observed.

Manuela disagreed. True, Berta was a little plump, but she had delicate features and such enviable skin. As for herself, Manuela, she thought she looked good. The mirror didn't lie: A fresh, girlish face, slender but shapely—in other words, a lovely woman!

3

They traveled by train with false passports, on a complicated, exhausting trip with many layovers and changes, until they got off at a station where a comrade was waiting for them. They recognized each other by the usual method. In this case, the comrade had his cap in his hand, and they had a specific newspaper in plain sight. He directed himself toward them, asking, "Are you coming from León?" They answered, "No, we came from Madrid."

Together they took a bus to a village where the comrade brought them to a cheap tavern, where he introduced them to another Portuguese, the man who was to be their guide crossing the border.

The guide reacted rudely, not expecting two women. It seemed to him, they would not be up to it. The route planned was over the rocky, steep desert Soajo mountain. It was a long and dangerous course, made more difficult by the luggage they were carrying. What a stupid idea, coming burdened like that. They wouldn't make it.

"We'll make it, don't worry," Manuela interrupted him.

The man shook his head and wouldn't speak, almost as if there was nothing more he could say.

"We can't stay here, my friend," Berta added. "We're already here, so you have to take us."

They all sat there stymied, not knowing what to do. Then the two men stepped aside for a few minutes to talk by themselves. They came back with their decision.

"The four of us will go together," said the man who had met them at the train.

"There's no other way to do it," the other agreed, annoyed and in foul mood. "But you two women are going to kill yourselves."

4

They hadn't even started to ascend the mountains before they were tired already. The suitcases, though not heavy, were not meant to be carried on such long hikes. They asked to stop and rest a little.

The men acceded, the guide, with his back turned toward the others, viewing the mountain range both close and far.

Farther ahead, traipsing across rocky, uneven ground with sharp drops, the two burdened women fell behind from time to time, obliging the men to stop and wait.

After an hour, Berta placed her suitcase on the ground and sat on a flat rock, breathing with difficulty. "It'll pass," she said to the others standing around her.

It did pass, but when she stood up, the comrade who waited for them at the train station grabbed her suitcase without saying a word and started walking right behind the guide.

The trail grew ever more steep, and the footwork even trickier. Manuela stopped often to set her suitcase down, not keeping up with the pace. For the third time, letting the men walk ahead, Berta stopped and waited for her. Manuela was almost crawling on the ascent.

"Give me your suitcase. I'll carry it for a while."

"Never mind, I've got it."

"No," Berta said firmly, "give it here!" And she practically tore it from Manuela's hands.

Up ahead, the guide had also stopped to survey the area. He waited for Berta to catch up, and without a word, just as she had done for Manuela, snatched the suitcase out of her hands, placed it on his shoulder and started marching again.

Another hour, and yet another. The guide stopped again, put Manuela's suitcase down, and waited for the others. They were way behind, and when he looked back, he saw them all seated on the ground, seemingly in conversation.

From that group, the comrade from the train station gave a hand signal to the guide to wait. Without rejoining the women, the comrade, too, waited.

Her feet all bloody and full of blisters, Manuela begged to rest and regain her energy. The pains were intense. Every step made her want to scream. Finally, she stood up impulsively. "Let's go!"

They all resumed the march. The comrade, with Berta's suitcase on his shoulder, walked dexterously. Berta dragged behind, supporting her limping friend.

The guide waited until they all reached him, looked at Manuela and spoke to her with an accusatory tone. "What did you expect would happen with those shoes? They may be good for the city, but not for a trek like this."

5

Crossing the range, with its mountains of bare rock, took many hours. It was a sad, forced march, where each one helped the others. Short pauses for rest relieved the hours and hours of climbing. The last two hours were the descent.

At the bottom they confronted a surprising spectacle. On an immense stone platform rose mysterious stone constructions in the shape of grain silos. Were they actual silos? Religious symbols? They stopped, admired and wondered. This was the designated spot for them to separate.

The Portuguese guide would proceed directly to the settlement not far away. The other comrade, consulting his watch, told the two women that just farther on there would be a car to pick them up.

The guide stood for another few moments watching his friends walk away.

Suddenly, Manuela, who was limping with Berta's help, turned back in an awkward run, with her bleeding feet hopping as if on hot coals. With her hand cordially on the guide's shoulder, she told him, smiling slyly, "So now, my friend, they say this isn't for women!"

She returned to join her comrades with the same clumsy gait, hopping as if on hot coals.

A few hundred meters on, a car waited for them by the side of the road. As if coming out to greet them, a warm ray of sun broke through the clouds and fell upon them.

Manuela turned to Berta. "Look at that sun, my friend! I could really have used that hat from the Brazilian comrade."

The Hold

1

IT was Blond Zé who suggested this solution. A welder at the Rocha shipyards, he delivered the news. The Azorean Company liner *Gonçalo Velho* had been sold to Yugoslavia and was at the shipyards for repairs, modernization, painting and change of name. It would be known as the *Yug*, and on the chimney they were painting an enormous red star. Most of the crew from Yugoslavia were already on board. Despite the permanent surveillance by the PIDE—the International and State Defense Police—whose teams of agents took turns on the ship, contact had been established between the shipyard workers and the crew. Stumbling through English and Spanish, Blond Zé managed to speak with a few of them.

"They're a good bunch of men. They asked if there was a party here and they asked for materials."

With that news transmitted, it was decided to pose the question: If it were possible to clandestinely transport a comrade who was being sent on a foreign mission. Blond Zé delivered the request and a response came back within a few days: They wanted to know more.

By appointment with a responsible comrade, a crew member appeared, presenting himself as the commissar on board. At the end of the conversation he said he could not decide on his own, but he would see that someone would give an answer through Blond Zé. Two weeks later, the response came. They asked for further information, but they did agree to take the comrade. Everything should be handled between Blond Zé and two of the seamen he knew, Miko and Pavelic.

It was projected that the liner would be ready to depart within two weeks. Beforehand, the ship would leave the channel to see if everything was working right. By that time, the comrade should already be on board, because it could be expected that the PIDE vigilance would intensify closer to departure time, and at that point it would be even harder for an unauthorized person to board the ship.

The best way to board would be to join up with a group of seamen and enter with them, as if returning from bingeing on the town. At the checkpoint he would show the identification card of another seaman who had remained on board.

And that's how they did it.

2

All went well. At the gangway, the PIDE agents barely looked at the sailors' ID cards, and Miko and Pavelic, stealing away from the other crew members, led Carlos to a cabin with a door onto a deck looking out over the open sea.

His first impressions couldn't have been better. Carlos never expected he'd be so well situated on this voyage, in a first-class stateroom with all the amenities and a private bathroom.

When the sailors left, he lay down comfortably and within a few minutes he was peacefully asleep.

Day had barely broken when Miko and Pavelic appeared, bringing a sandwich and coffee. But they were worried. They had just heard that PIDE was going to conduct a thorough inspection of the ship that morning. During the day it would be impossible to leave the cabin and take him to a more secure place. However, they concocted a plan and proceeded to execute it.

Dressed in the white jacket of a menial onboard staff member, with his face covered by lather, Carlos would pose as someone shaving, leaving the stateroom door open out to the deck. If the door were closed, it would more dangerous: The agents would open it in their search, ask questions, and that would be much worse. He had to maintain that pretense for as long as necessary, lathering up continuously until the PIDE had passed. They would figure he was part of the crew and would continue their inspection. If they directed any question to him, he should make some gesture of not understanding.

They practiced the scene, and with the door wide open to the deck, Miko and Pavelic went away.

It was risky and nerve-racking, but what else could he do? The foam dried, and he refreshed it several times, leaning into the mirror, in a repetitious manner that made him think of a clown slapstick. It took a long time, but the moment finally arrived. Incredibly, the PIDE men came along, looked curiously inside the cabin, saw the shaving in progress and continued on their way.

Their passing had been so quick that Carlos was not sure it was even the announced inspection. So whether it was or not, he continued the show and was almost surprised when Miko and Pavelic appeared, confirming that the search had concluded.

The incident proved that he could not remain in the cabin. There were still several days before departure, and the police would end up seeing him. They were frustrated, and begged his pardon, but that night they would have to move him to another place.

3

Leaving the stateroom, they quickly walked down the deck until once again entering the ship's interior. Through an open, metal-plated door, they entered an area with no light. With a flashlight pointing forward, they made innumerable turns down corridors, through hatchways, and down stairs.

Enveloped in darkness, they finally softened their footsteps, following the beam from Miko's flashlight, elbowing their way through bulky volumes of freight on the immense, wide, flat wooden floor of the hold.

They stopped. The two seamen exchanged a few words that Carlos did not understand, they took hold of him, lifted him up and helped him to jump atop a wall of packing crates, pointed the flashlight into an empty space that looked more than anything else like a well, and helped him drop into it to the bottom.

Light from the flashlight still faintly illuminated the space above his open hiding place in the middle of the cargo. Then the glimmer faded away and everything went dark and silent.

By feel, Carlos recognized what, by agreement, they had left there for him. A pail, a blanket, a bottle of water, a package of food that they tossed in when they arrived. All as planned, everything in order. But immediately he found it unbearable— the forced inertia, the darkness and silence, this prison in an unknown spot somewhere in the vast entrails of the ship. He had no reference to the passage of time, no possibility whatsoever of leaving from there, nor any idea or any way to know when they would come to get him.

Though time began to pass, it seemed it wasn't passing at all. He couldn't tell if it was transpiring quickly or slowly. He didn't know if he had been in that hole a quarter of an hour, or an hour, or only a few minutes. Deprived of any agency, he was condemned to wait quietly in silence and in darkness.

4

So he remained, seated on the floor, immobile and inert for a timeless time. Minutes? Hours? He would never know. As time went on, time went on—beyond measure, eyes closed, eyes open without seeing anything, in endless waiting.

A sudden burst of initiative seized him. He stood up, raised an arm and stretched it high to see how deep was his hiding place. Then he felt from corner to corner, measuring the space palm by palm. He sat down again, setting the pail, the blanket, the food package and the bottle against one of the crates.

And once again, in that hole, in the dark silence, he felt the terrifying incapacity to decide. He was totally, absolutely dependent on others, entirely at their mercy. Memories and pictures came to him persistently—of his meeting with Blond Zé and the sailors on a city street, the group walking along the dock, going up in single file to the checkpoint, the PIDE agents looking at the IDs, the stateroom and the shaving scene, the PIDE agents' inspection, the wild traverse through corridors, hatches and stairs until they brought him to this hole in the hull. The images piled one on top of another, but clean and clear as though he were reliving all those moments. With his legs extended, his back and head against the crates, his eyes closed, picture after picture after picture, he fell asleep.

For how long—seconds? Minutes? Hours? He awoke as though he had not been asleep, with a lucid sense of the situation in which he found himself. But now he felt cold, very cold. He reached for the blanket, wrapped himself in it and stretched out. Before long, he was asleep again.

5

Waking again, he had no way of knowing how long he had slept, whether a lot or a little. He sat up, still leaning against the crates, and snuggled up with his blanket. He felt more inertly dazed than anxious, eyes open only to see nothing in the complete dark, worrying about the passage of time. Then another bolt of initiative struck, a will to act.

He felt for the substantial food package and started unwrapping it with curiosity, almost with pleasure. With his eyes useless in the darkness, his other senses revealed the form and image of the things which sight would have given him but now couldn't. Touch, smell and taste came into service, all contributing to his understanding of what he had.

First of all, a big loaf of bread, with a hardy crust and a soft, tasty body, certainly a white bread. Then something heavy, long, cylindrical and round, wrapped in noisy paper as he opened it. One bite gave off the intense aroma of smoked meat, maybe a mortadella, he guessed, a reddish, mottled salt pork. Or maybe a sausage of mixed meats, a salmagundi. His adventure of discovery proceeded with palpable enthusiasm. There was something else, too, limp and lukewarm, wrapped in parchment paper. It almost wasn't necessary to unwrap it—he had only to smell and lick it. Hooray! It was a roast chicken.

His discovery complete, he arranged the items in a row, one after the other, to easily find them. Once in order, the novel idea came to him that this was food to eat—and with that, the revelation that he was hungry. He had no idea how much time he had been there, if it was day or night, or what time of day or night, or how many days since he had boarded the ship. He ate hungrily. A piece of bread that he judged of good quality, a tasty chicken leg and, after hesitating, a wing that he ripped off with some difficulty. Sips of water accompanied his meal. Just one problem: His hands all greasy, with nowhere to wipe them clean. Oh, well, he couldn't have everything. He wiped his hands above him on the cargo containers and then finished off with a corner of the blanket as a towel: cleanliness as circumstance allowed.

After this series of events, he was happy and refreshed. He fell asleep, and woke up again. And again and again. Then he ate some more. There were empty times, too, of waiting and anticipation. So it continued for an interminable time. Silence and darkness, silence, darkness, silence, darkness.

6

Carlos was drifting somewhere between drowsiness and sleep when, out of the interminable, shapeless night, his ears perked up to a sudden sound.

Someone was walking through the hold, with slight noises at first, but growing more perceptible and nearer, and finally very audible. A faint light cut across the top circumference of his hiding place, the first sign of light in his unaccountable time of darkness.

In another moment, from above, sharply and brutally, came a beam of light from the flashlight that hurt his eyes.

Then he saw two indistinct faces and an extended arm that demanded the grasp of his hand. On his feet now, supported and rocking uncertainly in his gait behind the flashlight beam, he followed in his companions' rapid footsteps. Through the hold they walked, winding between crates of cargo, until they mounted a steep staircase, then another and another, emerging from the dark into the fresh air of night dotted with the fairyland lights of docks and ships.

Was his torture of darkness and silence in the hold over? A brief illusion.

More steps, and once again the flashlight, more stairs, more hatchways, into the bowels of the ship. Metal staircases, corridors, echoing spaces, more stairs. And strangely, absurdly, after having ascended so much, now the general direction of their route was not going up but going down. They descended more and more until they got to a weird, wide, empty and cold space with a curved floor, smelling intensely of oil. The focus of the flashlight was aimed at the floor. His companions helped him lie at an awkward angle against a metal plate.

They handed him a blanket and said a few words, of which he understood only, "We'll come back to get you!" The flashlight beam retreated from view and disappeared, and he was left again in the dark, but now in an even more terrible place. In any direction he extended his arms, he felt nothing but the cold metallic surface. It wasn't long before he realized that the hull against which they placed him was below the waterline. The frigid cold of the metal armature passed into his body, and every now and then, from above, he heard the gurgle of water lapping at the shell of the ship.

7

Almost like a shocking explosion, a deafening noise accompanied by vibration on the metal hull set into motion the shaking of the whole ocean liner. The transmission shaft and the propeller blades had been engaged, very close to him. The intense, aggressive sound beat and assaulted the inside of his head. Carlos grabbed the blanket and wrapped his head in it, covering his ears as hard as he could in self-defense. It seemed it would never stop. But after a while, once the initial jolt had passed, the noise did seem to diminish.

An easy, repeated, cadenced rocking told him the ship was sailing. Surely, as they had told him, this was the trial run into the sea. The rocking became greater and greater, his part of the ship rose and fell, rose and fell, sometimes energetically. They must have passed the channel.

Thinking this must be the final test before departure, it was less difficult for him through the next few hours, lying against the cold metal incline, in total darkness, cowering and trembling from the cold, hands over his ears, the blanket rolled around his head. Remaining in that position, he had the impression they were returning to port, through the channel entrance, and sailing up the Tagus River to dock. Then, the maneuvers of docking and shutting down the propellers, with only the sound of the motors in operation, which now sounded almost gentle.

They came to get him and led him once again to his hiding place in the hold. More time in the dark, without end, that could not be measured, recommenced.

The comrades showed up, but on the run, twice more, bringing more food and water. He ate, slept and woke up many times, without calendar or clock. Until once more the sounds of the motors and propellers, and the rocking of the ship, gave him the picture of sailing down the Tagus, passing through the channel, and entering the open sea. But no one appeared. Would he make the whole voyage in that hole?

But no. Miko and Pavelic came with their flashlight, and walking back through the same course, led him to his stateroom. They were relaxed and laughing.

In Spanish and English, they congratulated him. Finally he was free.

8

In the stateroom where he was installed, Carlos lacked for nothing—tasty meals and friendly visitors. Clearly they wanted to make up for the difficult test he had endured. They only asked him not to leave the cabin, as only a few members of the crew knew there was a clandestine passenger aboard.

During those days on the ocean, Miko and Pavelic stopped by several times, as well as the onboard commissar who had met with the party comrade in Lisbon.

In a mélange of Spanish and English, they managed to explain why things had gone in such an unexpected and happenstance way. They had counted on the liner leaving a week after he was on board, right after the last test run out of the channel and onto the open sea. The ship was delayed making the trial run, and then not everything was exactly right, and they had to solve those issues.

When the ship left the harbor out to sea, when they took him out of the hold and brought him down to the ship's hull, that was because, at the last minute, the PIDE demanded that the hold be disinfected, which would compromise his safety in the hiding place they had prepared for him.

The voyage met with calm seas and good sailing. When they came to his cabin to bring meals or converse a little, they informed him of their progress. That they had passed through the Strait of Gibraltar, entered the Mediterranean, were navigating past Sicily and into the Adriatic. Finally, to great excitement, the *Yug* arrived at the port of Split.

The commissar came to the stateroom, to affirm that he, for his part, had completed his duty, and to say goodbye. He also said that comrades from the party were waiting for him. They would proceed by train to Zagreb, and then to Belgrade. Everything would be taken care of according to the request made of them.

* * *

In Lisbon, a comrade happened to run into Blond Zé, the welder at the Rocha shipyards who had made the contact with the seamen.

"Zé, do you have any news of those friends? Have they returned to port?" Already a month had passed—it was about time the comrade would be returning, and they had no news.

"Returning?" Blond Zé replied in shock. "The ship just left a week ago."

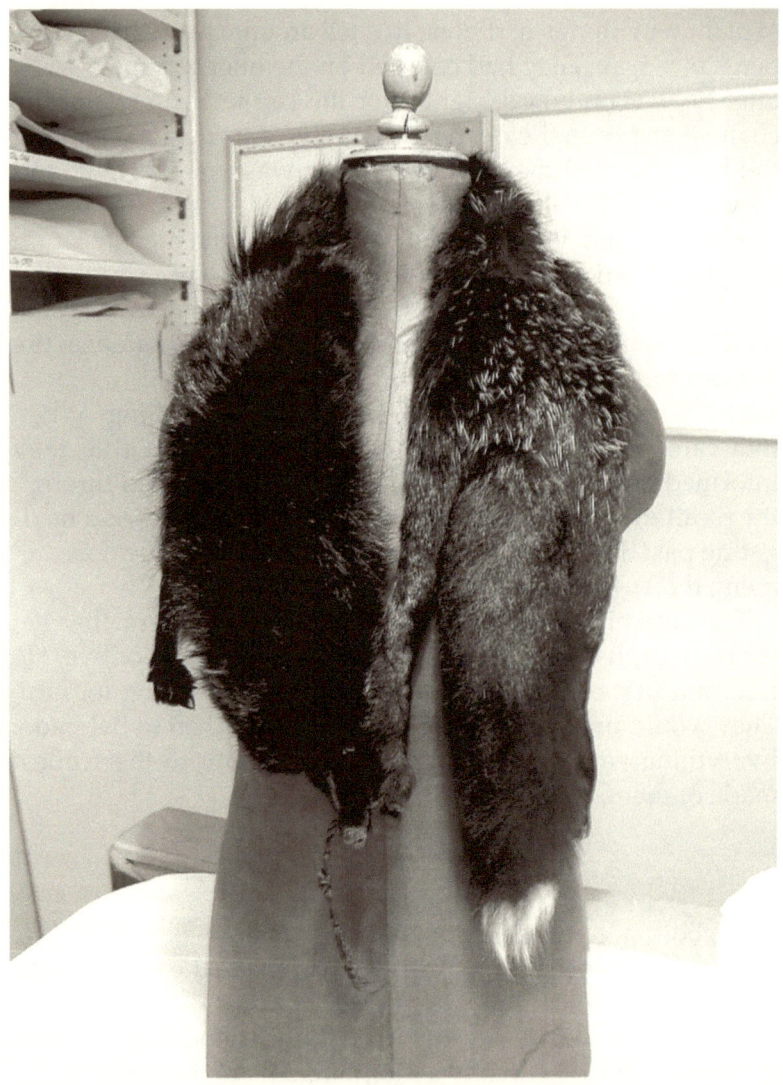

Woman's black fox fur stole complete with head, tail, paws, lined with brown silk, 1930s (Auckland War Memorial Museum), Creative Commons

The Suitcase with Luxury Furs

VIRIATO completed a highly specialized course: preparation for guerrilla warfare, manufacture of explosives, mines and booby traps. Now he had to get back to his country. Just on the eve of his departure, he was assigned a new task, to go through nearby countries. Every aspect of his departure had been carefully studied and readied, and all very much in a hurry.

In his room he left a suitcase full of notes and materials from the course for a comrade in his training camp to fetch after a few days. He also arranged another suitcase with personal things—toiletries, ladies undergarments and souvenirs for his wife—for another comrade who would be returning legally to their home country with it,.

"Watch out you don't lose it along the way," he advised. But ideally, it would be better if the suitcase evaded a search by Customs—not on account of the underwear, but rather a fur hat and stole he had bought her. Over here they were cheap, but in Portugal they'd be worth a fortune.

"For you, it should be no problem," he added. "But since the export of furs is not allowed without a license, they could seize them. That would be a shame."

"If you don't mind the risk of losing them," the comrade assured him, "for me, it won't be a problem."

So he said, but it was with a certain nervousness that he took charge of the bag. It wouldn't be pleasant if they confiscated the furs from him. Viriato trusted him, but the furs were valuable, and who knows what he would think.

At Customs the next day, he had his first shock. In front of him, they were arguing with a woman about a fox fur they found in her suitcase. He didn't understand what they were saying, but it was a prolonged discussion. *I'm screwed*, he thought, his hand gripping the suitcase handle. The guard, however, so as not to hold up the line, signaled him to come to the front and proceed through on his way.

The rest of the trip went smoothly. At different Customs stations, he experienced the same moments of nervousness. But in every case, they told him to proceed, and never checked his baggage. "I must have the face of a respectable person," he chuckled to himself.

When he arrived back home, he asked his comrades to deliver the suitcase to Viriato's wife.

"Women's underthings and some luxury furs. Make sure there's no mix-up or that it doesn't get forgotten."

"Don't worry, it will be delivered."

The porter went to see Viriato's wife, handed her the suitcase and left.

After a few days, a furor broke out. The troubled woman contacted every person she could think of.

She had opened the suitcase and what she found appalled her. Notebooks with lessons from Viriato's course, drawings, formulas, photos of guns, grenades and other weapons, and even electrical equipment, wires and other highly suspect materials.

What a disaster. The comrade had picked up the suitcase meant to go to the training camp, and left the other one with the furs and women's underthings.

As for the first suitcase, a comrade took it away and, following instructions from his superiors, dumped it into the ocean at an appropriate spot.

As for the other, no one ever found out what the reaction by the instructors at the training camp was. Was someone severely chastised? Or did they open the bag to general hilarity, seeing the furs and unfolding and holding up the women's undergarments?

It's easy to imagine the scene, but impossible to know.

Overview of the city of Geneva. Werner Friedli, June 1947 (Creative Commons)

In Brazen Pursuit

1

BEFORE he returned to his country Alberto was given numerous, repeated pieces of advice.

He should maintain high vigilance because, with the responsibility he had, he was certain to be on file with the border police. His passport was in good order; still, however, it was false. He should rigorously follow the established itinerary because, in case of any adversity, they would be sure to try and find him and take appropriate measures. They added a number of other useful points and recommendations.

In Vienna, Austria, all went well at the airport control. He ate a schnitzel at a bar, strolled through the city, and that night boarded a train for Switzerland. He went through normal passport control with no special attention or notice.

In the morning, when he got off the train at the Zurich station, a first suspicion captured his attention.

On the platform, in the reverse direction from that of the scurrying, just arriving passengers, a man in a gabardine coat

with its collar raised, walking casually as if in studied natural-
ness, was obliquely eyeing everyone, practically one by one.
He looked at Alberto, too, with a slight turn of his head in
Alberto's direction and a quick, piercing stare. From his long
experience in the underground, Alberto was certain that that
man did not just look at him as he did everyone else, but that
he recognized him. More than that, that the man was looking for him in the Zurich train station, upon his arrival on the
express from Vienna.

The train to Geneva was leaving in an hour. He purchased
newspapers and tobacco and had a coffee. The man had
disappeared.

But on the departure platform, when he reached his car on
the Zurich-Geneva express, there he was, standing in the middle of all the passenger foot traffic, now in the company of
another. Once again, Alberto caught a furtive glance.

I don't like this, he thought.

2

The trip to Geneva proceeded uneventfully, however, with
nothing that aroused Alberto's attention.

A lively French-speaking family were his compartment companions, a married couple and a young woman. They talked
constantly about what had occurred over the past few days,
about such-and-such a coat that caught their eye in a store, or
a dish they had eaten in a restaurant. A film, or an argument
they were witness to on a bus, things of that sort.

The curious part of it was that, whatever they talked about,
their opinions were all different. If the man had one, the
younger woman had another, and the wife, seeking to smooth
over the differences, wound up defending both views. There
was a great deal of discussion about a dog they had seen and
liked.

"That St. Bernard was soooo cute," the young woman said.

"It wasn't a St. Bernard," the man corrected. "It was a
Newfoundland."

"Not so, Papa," she insisted. "It was definitely a St. Bernard,
you can be positive."

"You both are right," the wife remarked. The tail, she explained, was in fact that of a St. Bernard, but the hair was of a Newfoundland.

Up to that time, Alberto had not exchanged a single word with them. Unexpectedly, they asked him to enter the fray.

"This gentleman will decide," said the daughter.

And without waiting for his response, she described the features of its ears and its snout, the color and texture of its hair, the size and shape of its body and tail, asking him to make the final decision.

Alberto knew almost nothing about dogs. He couldn't give an opinion.

"What?!" the young woman exclaimed indignantly. Couldn't he recognize the difference? Shocking!

From that point, a certain compartmental relationship flowered. Someone offered a cigarette, loaned a newspaper. And the animated conversation among the family members continued.

As their accent was somewhat unfamiliar to Alberto, he inquired what region of France they were from.

The man laughed. "We are not French, we are Swiss."

Swiss? Alberto had always heard the Swiss were such reserved people, and remarked as such.

The man laughed again. "People from Zurich, yes. But we're from Bern."

They left their names and address with Alberto and invited him to visit them if he ever passed through again. They left, saying their goodbyes from the platform.

Alberto rode alone in the compartment on to Geneva.

3

At the end of the trip in Geneva he saw nothing strange. Since the train for Paris departed only at night, he decided to walk through the city and have dinner somewhere. He took in the beauty of the big lake and the panorama of distant, snow-covered mountains and enjoyed a delicious, leisurely dinner. Everything appeared normal.

Leaving the restaurant, he encountered a new twist. At the door three standing men quickly shifted their position, turning their backs toward him as he passed.

Cops, undoubtedly, cops, he thought. *Here comes the chase scene.*

In fact, that's just what started, a race through the streets. Him, cutting them off at the corner, them in hot pursuit. When he thought he had evaded them, the three reappeared, generally standing, pretending they didn't see him. At the end, the hunted one showed his superior skill. Near the lake, in the narrow streets of the old city, he succeeded in throwing them off his trail.

Whew! he thought. *That wasn't easy!*

With the departure time nearing for the train to Paris, he decided to walk to the station, still checking to see if he were being followed. He didn't see anything suspect. He seated himself in the cafeteria with a great sense of relief. But his respite did not last long. A few minutes later, looking around, he saw that his three hunters had sat down at the very next table, the same guys who had followed him out of the restaurant.

Anxious again, he passed through customs and passport control. He found his train, his car, and his seat, and occupied it still in a worrisome state. He had good reason. Before the train started off, looking out onto the platform, he saw those same three pursuers talking together right outside his window.

4

Alberto reported what happened and the issue was analyzed. Was it a matter of passage through Switzerland of suspects coming from Eastern Europe?

His comrades did not think that probable. The Swiss were bored already with the knowledge that Zurich was a favorite layover for revolutionaries from all over the world who visited the Soviet Union. It was hard to prove if it was true or merely anecdotal, but the story was told about one time, when they searched the baggage of some passenger arriving from a distant country, and they found a heavy weapon rolled up in clothing. There was no diplomatic fuss or anything. The customs employee put everything back as it was and signaled for the passenger to board. Obviously following higher orders.

What happened with Alberto was most unusual, but it did not appear to have anything to do with the Swiss.

His story was told and retold many times. Only much later did the explanation emerge.

On a delegation to the country from which Alberto had returned to Portugal, the hosts, who had never heard what happened, revealed the mystery.

Given the high responsibility of this comrade, they had organized his return trip with exacting care. They gave him thorough advice and set his itinerary. They had also given instruction to their own people that, at each stage of the trip, they should make sure the comrade proceeded without incident. And not just that. But to do it discreetly, as best possible without exposing themselves, and to be ready to assist with any serious problem that might come up. But discreetly, as they were charged.

Friedrichstrasse Station, Berlin, 1932 (FOTO:FORTEPAN/MZSL/Ofner Károly), Creative Commons

By Train Through Nazi Germany

1

BRIGHT, enterprising, always ready for any assignment, Vito, despite his youth, was sent to the Soviet Union.

It was a risky trip—secretive border crossings by foot from Portugal into Spain and from Spain to France. Then, by rail, with a false passport, he crossed Nazi Germany, through the Danzig Corridor, East Prussia and the Baltic countries to Moscow.

He attended a course, got to know the country a little, and now he was set to return.

Traversing Germany once again would be more dangerous than the trip east. They took into consideration, however, that Vito had a knack for wriggling out of any situation. Carrying a French passport, he spoke French perfectly—at least according to himself. He was shameless and full of spunk, and prepared to assume any risk. The way he spontaneously received the news of his departure ruled out any last-minute second thoughts.

A comrade accompanied him discreetly to the train, showed him his car and seat, and left him to his own devices.

2

The compartment had two beds, which would be opened up at night. He had just arranged his suitcase when the other passenger arrived. A tall, thin man, he appeared from his features and his clothing to be a foreigner. To confirm it, a tag hanging from his bag indicted his name: P. Brown.

A hostess in a green uniform and a red star on her képi came in to place two glasses of hot tea on the little table next to the window. Transparent and reflecting the light, it glistened through the decorative metal holder. Vito drank it right away, grateful for it. The indifferent Brown sat looking out the window. Soon, a whistle sounded and the train rumbled out, slowly and heaving at first, the boiler blowing rhythmically into the immense void of the station. Then, to the sharp squeal of the wheels switching onto successive tracks, the train advanced through interminable city buildings. Finally, it was rolling rapidly, jostling *tum-tum*, *tum-tum*, through the endless Russian plains edged by forest.

After prolonged silence in the compartment, a conversation finally began.

"Do you speak English?" Brown asked. "Do you understand?"

"Yes, yes, I do," Vito responded.

Brown spoke fast and, when it seemed that Vito was not comprehending, he turned to Russian.

"*Vy ponimaete?*"

"*Da, da, ponimayu,*" Vito answered. Yes, I understand.

Not that he liked to brag, but for Vito foreign languages were child's play. Spanish, of course, for all Portuguese, at least so the Portuguese believed. French—as if he were a Frenchman!, one of his comrades told him. English, he had studied in school. For German, he bought *German Without Pain* when he knew he'd be passing through Germany, and studied it eagerly, happily discovering its simple phonetics. Russian he learned not only from books, but from the intense intimacy he shared during his sojourn with the Soviets, above all with the girls.

So he had no difficulty. After two hours, he ended up knowing everything about his traveling companion.

He was an English engineer. He worked at a metallurgical combine in Chelyabinsk in the Urals. Now he was going home to England on vacation. He was one of the survivors of the Arctic catastrophe of the RA-101, the Italian dirigible under Nobile's command. He was saved, along with other castaways, by the Soviets, and he remained in the USSR to work ever since. Life was all right there but, judging from his words, nothing worked. "*Naprimer, kotleta,*" he said. "Cutlets, for example. All the time! Do you like a cutlet?"

From his tone, Vito realized in that moment that he was not speaking with a friend, indeed very far from that.

"*Vy pravda,*" Vito answered. "You're right, it's terrible."

So he said, but the truth is that Vito really loved a fine cutlet, especially accompanied by sautéed potatoes and little pickled cucumbers.

"It's terrible" was the magic phrase that gained Brown's confidence.

The conversation continued. So if he was French, as Vito said, what was he doing in the Soviet Union? He had an easy, ready response to that, as his passport indicated. He was a theater artist. It was a research trip. And how was the Soviet theater? Now Vito had a ready response to everything.

"It's terrible! The French theater is better!"

Brown was not happy with that response. "The English theater is the best in the world," he pronounced in English, and that put an end to the conversation.

3

Brown was reading a newspaper as Vito watched the scenery when, from the passageway, perceptibly through the powerful, sometimes earsplitting clatter of the train in motion, the crooning of a well-known revolutionary song came to the compartment. Vito's ears perked up. No question about it, someone was singing.

He couldn't resist and got up to look. He was not mistaken. At the end of the corridor, the only passenger in view, a tall, gangly man, was singing the "Partisan" song. *This guy is crazy*, Vito thought. And it was in fact craziness, on a train from Moscow to Berlin.

The man turned around, saw Vito, and was not flustered, but kept on singing. Two mischievous eyes shone out of his sallow, freckled face, as if to say, *Yes, I'm singing a song you know. And what of it?* After a moment he stopped, approached Vito and asked for a light.

"Polish!" he explained, pointing a finger at himself. "*Ya polyak, ponimaesh?*"

Without answer as to whether or not he understood, Vito lit the man's cigarette. The man went back to where he had come from, leaning against the window watching the landscape and picking up the next verse of his song.

Vito retreated back to his compartment. Did that man realize the risk he was taking? Was he really Polish, and where was he headed? If he was a Communist, which one could assume from the song, he certainly wouldn't be going to Germany. After East Prussia, the train would cross the Danzig Corridor—Polish territory—but the train didn't make a stop there. Was he going to jump from the train in motion? Vito thought better of going out to the corridor again and getting into conversation with the Pole.

Half an hour later, the man passed in front of the compartment. Through the door open to the corridor, he looked in and, for some brief seconds, Vito caught his glance fixed on him, observing. He pretended not to have noticed. By his side, the Englishman continued reading his newspaper.

4

At the border, the Soviet guard, slowly and calmly, with barely a word, walked through each carriage, checked passports, and half an hour later the train started moving again.

After another half hour, with a hair-raising screech of the brakes, the train rolled alongside the platform of a spacious station. As soon as it stopped, the cars were invaded by Nazi guards. With their swastika armbands and orders barked out incomprehensibly, they forced the passengers to line up in the carriage corridors and then dismount, still in line, on the platform. There they stood in formation, framed by rows of provocatively watchful guards.

The police control was installed right on the platform. As the passengers stepped out from the line, they handed over their passports, answered questions, got their passports stamped and were led back into the cars, where Nazi guards remained in the passageways.

It was a disquieting spectacle in and of itself. But Vito, in his own way, observed little details as though they were cartoons—the bulging belly of one guard so out of character with his military posture, the expression of another, with his mustache like Hitler's, that crowd of guards, more than there were passengers, surrounding them as if they were prisoners of war.

When it was his turn, he handed over his passport and the officer shot several questions at him. Name? Vito responded quickly. Right. Nationality? French, he responded with assurance. Right.

The third question he didn't entirely understand, but he deduced it had to do with his age, and confident of his knowledge of German, pertly said, "*Drei und zwanzig!*" Twenty-three!

A virtual storm broke out. The officer pointed to the passport and repeated his question several more times. Without understanding what was causing such a hubbub, Vito kept repeating his response, though less confidently now. "*Drei und zwanzig.*"

His face registering deep consternation, the police officer stood up and showed the passport to one of his colleagues, pointing in it to something or other.

Then a policewoman, also part of the control team and obviously a translator, came to Vito and said to him, quite amiably, "*On vous a demandé combien de jours vous resterez à Berlin.*" How many days would he be staying in Berlin?

"Oh! I misunderstood," Vito responded in French. He explained that he thought they were asking his age, adding that he'd be in Berlin only a day to see the city and would continue on as soon as possible to Paris.

She translated for her colleague, who grunted something which by its tone must have been either a curse or an insult, and returned the passport.

Mad and annoyed at himself, Vito was led back to his carriage and compartment. Shortly after, they brought Brown.

5

Pulling out of the border station, the train picked up speed all through East Prussia. Brown's mood changed abruptly. "Goodbye, *tovarishchi!*" he said apropos of nothing, but clearly disparagingly of "comrades."

With some odd moves, he unbuckled his pants belt, located a hidden pocket inside his trousers, and took out two envelopes. In a theatrical gesture he kissed one, then the other.

"Now we're safe, my friend!" he said to Vito, reverting to English, in a triumphant inflection.

"Yes, yes," Vito answered blandly, not knowing what to say.

Maybe the train would stop at Königsberg. From there to Berlin it would still be several more hours.

Unexpectedly, a new passenger entered the compartment. He did not explain why he came there, not having an assigned place. Uniformed, with a swastika on his armband, he said not a word. He sat in a corner next to the passageway door, and kept looking at them with an astonished glare.

This guy is here to watch us like two wild animals coming out of the Soviet Union, Vito thought, and considered taking a nap. But he couldn't. Whenever he opened his eyes, he noticed the Nazi sitting in his corner, not having once changed position, with one enormous eye open and unblinking, staring at him fixedly.

It looks like a glass eye, Vito surmised, finding once again the comical in the image.

It happened time after time: Vito opened his eyes, and they landed on the Nazi in the corner, his enormous, terrifying eye alert and steady. Evidently, he did not wish to fall asleep. Why? To keep watch? Was he afraid? Imagining the fear that bug-eyed Nazi must have been living with in the presence of two presumed Bolsheviks coming from the USSR, Vito surprised even himself by finding an excuse to laugh, thinking about crossing Nazi Germany with the Gestapo on all sides surveilling the travelers and primed to intervene.

6

Staff members came to open up the beds. The Nazi intruder left at that point and didn't come back. Brown installed himself on the upper bunk without even asking Vito's preference. Stretched out with his head toward the window, Vito watched the scenery go by, monotonous, dun-colored and sad.

The express forged ahead with the insistent, deafening metallic noise of movement, with rhythmically repeating bursts of steam from the smokestack and from time to time, whistles to warn of the train's approach. Unexpectedly, the forward movement slowed down in a dark stretch with no visible lights, easing gradually until coming to a full stop in an almost absolute and disturbing silence. Inside, the train was completely quiet, and from outside, only the heavy panting from the boiler broke the silence. While the train was stopped, it seemed time had stopped, too. Then, slowly, ever so slowly, the train began to move again until it arrived at a small, almost deserted station. No one got off. On the platform, some railway workers, almost as if oblivious, barely glanced at the express which had just stopped there unscheduled. There the train sat, with no apparent reason for its stop.

Suddenly, rupturing the relative silence and tranquility, the beat of footsteps could be heard, at first on the platform, then in the carriage passageways. Compartment doors opened and closed, more footsteps advanced with the heavy stomping of whoever it was out in the corridor. No one spoke, no one said anything, as compartment doors opened and closed.

Finally they appeared—three or four SS men with rapid, decisive movements. They opened the door brusquely, turned on the light, and without saying a word, looked closely at the two passengers for a few seconds. Again without a word, they shut the light, closed the door and proceeded.

Once, twice, three times more, they heard the steps, a pause, the door opening, another pause, the door closing, always wordlessly. The fourth was different. At the sound of the door opening, voices broke out, an argument with an elevated tone, a shout, and then a huge commotion that shortly spilled out of the car.

Rising from his bed, Vito saw the group leaving the train, then on the platform. The SS guards were holding and pushing the Polish man who, taller than the others, turned his head from side to side like a trapped crane. Vito saw the Pole twisting himself and making a sudden effort to stop. The SS quickly pushed him through a door into the interior of the station.

On the platform, only a few railway workers and policemen remained. No one appeared to have witnessed the scene.

"What's going on?" a startled Brown asked from his upper bunk.

"Nothing, nothing," Vito replied.

Only now did he become fully aware just how real the dangers of his trip were. He saw Brown pull two envelopes out of the false pocket in his pants. He recalled the stupid response he had given in German to the Gestapo without knowing what he was saying. And the Nazi with one eye closed and the other always open. And the Polish guy, with the foxy look in his eyes as he sang the "Partisan," and then the SS shoving him off the train and disappearing him into the station.

In Berlin, he said goodbye to Brown, took a stroll around the city and boarded the first available train for Paris.

7

A passenger in street clothes who sat next to him, seeing that Vito was reading a book in French, asked him courteously if he was French. Vito confirmed it, and his seat mate observed that he didn't have a Parisian accent. Was he from the north or the south?

"*Je suis de Nantes*," I'm from Nantes, he replied, the birthplace listed on his passport.

"Ah," the other man replied, "is that north or south of Paris?"

In truth, Vito didn't know. But he found a way out of answering. As if he considered the question absurd, he responded with a chuckle, "It's on the Mediterranean coast in the Normandy sun."

"Ah," the other man repeated, and after a short time, left the compartment.

I fooled you! Vito thought for a moment before he stopped ruminating any more about it. But walking into the dining car, another surprise awaited him. In the booth where the Gestapo agents had ostentatiously installed themselves, chatting with other uniformed agents was that same passenger from Vito's compartment in civilian clothes.

From then on, everything seemed suspect. There was the fat woman who came and stopped in the passageway right in front of his compartment. There was the passenger who passed by his door three times, and even the long look from the conductor.

But nothing more happened for the rest of the trip. At the French border station, the Nazi police left, and the French train crew took over.

In Paris, one of Vito's French comrades made a comment that stirred him to reflect more deeply on what he had experienced.

It was just a few months ago, the comrade reported, that two Latin American comrades who, like Vito, had traveled from Moscow through Germany with false passports disappeared during the trip and nothing further had been heard of them.

Geneva, Gare de Cornavin (Werner Friedli, 1953), Creative Commons

Comrade and Gentleman

IN Geneva, customs and passport control were both located right in the railway station, Swiss and French, one after the other. From one to the other, before your train left, you got into the customs line and calmly waited your turn. You only had to say, "Nothing to declare," and they told you to proceed. Half a dozen steps later, the Swiss police looked at your passport, and then the French did the same. You went to the platform, boarded the train, looked for your assigned seat, and that was it. Then you just waited for the departure, and within minutes you were already traveling through French territory without any further police control problems.

Bernardo knew all this because it had all been explained before the trip. It always worked that way with many others, and it would surely work the same way with him too.

Arriving early at the station, luggage in hand, Bernardo got into line and waited. Ahead of him, still at some distance from Customs, stood a few dozen people. Behind him, the queue extended out to the front door. He happened to be standing behind an attractive woman dressed with a certain elegance.

After a good half hour of tiresome delay, the line finally started moving. The woman lifted her suitcase from the floor and after a single step put it down again. She was slender, and the suitcase was obviously heavy. When the line advanced a little more, she dragged her suitcase with great difficulty, bent over by the effort and nearly losing her balance. Conscious, perhaps, of the scene she was creating, she turned back for the first time to see if anyone noticed, almost begging pardon for her awkwardness. She had a lovely, youthful face with fine features and a warm look about her.

Up to the Customs desk, Bernardo was helping the likable lady. In response to each of his gestures of assistance, she turned around and smiled. Anticipating that she would be unable to lift her suitcase to the counter, Bernardo naturally helped her do it. He thought it might earn him some credit. He thought, too, that by such a gesture, he would show the Customs agents how comfortable and at ease he felt. She thanked him, with an *oof!* of relief and another smile. She was pretty indeed.

There was general shock when she opened her suitcase— one, two, three, ten boxes of Swiss chocolates and several more chocolate blocks. Underneath a layer of clothes, yet another stash of chocolate.

The agents removed everything from the suitcase and placed it on the counter.

They quietly asked her if she knew it was prohibited to carry such a large quantity of chocolate. She reacted with patent surprise. No, she didn't know. Relatives and friends had begged her to bring them Swiss chocolate, and so she did.

It took a while. The clerk went to consult with his superior. When he returned, to Bernardo's surprise, he placed the chocolates back in the suitcase, helped her repack the clothes, and with a beatific, almost friendly wave, told her to proceed.

With his suitcase in hand, Bernardo was prepared to move straight through. "*Rien à déclarer!*" he said confidently. Nothing to declare.

That was the customary phrase they had advised him to say. "Your valise, *monsieur, s'il vous plaît,*" the clerk retorted.

Well, he had been told it was not usual for them to inspect the luggage, but what could he do? He placed the suitcase on the counter, and compliantly lifted the lid.

At first, their meticulous search seemed ridiculous to him, even disrespectful. The clerk unfolded every shirt, every pair of underwear, and every pair of socks. He opened and unceremoniously dumped out his toilette bag, with his razor, brush and soap stick, and squeezed his tube of toothpaste so hard that the cap flew off and the contents shot out like a long strand of spaghetti all over the counter.

"You're traveling with madame—" said the clerk.

"What?" a startled Bernardo answered. No, he had nothing to do with "madame" and her chocolates.

The clerk glanced ironically at the colleague beside him. Immediately, with a knife in his hand that he had pulled out from who knows where, he placed the point on the fabric lining of the suitcase. Now Bernardo happened to appreciate that lining very much, handsome, with pockets, dividers, belts and buckles. *Whss, whss!* The clerk cut it and ripped it from one side to the other, exposing the exterior casing of imitation leather plastic.

Bernardo was speechless.

They asked for his passport, and the clerk brazenly demanded further, what was his relationship with madame? Were they traveling together? Did he work with her? At the end of this outrageous show, as if all had been entirely normal and correct, they handed the passport back, haphazardly threw everything back in the suitcase, and without another word, signaled him to proceed.

Dumbfounded, he passed through the police without incident, walked down the platform, found his carriage compartment and assigned seat and, exhausted and dripping with sweat, sat there confused and fixed in place. What bizarre things happen!

The story was not over, however.

He was having a hard time dealing with what they did to him and closed his eyes. He was aroused by a sweet voice. It was the woman with the suitcase.

"*Vous permettez, Monsieur?* If it's all right with you, if there are empty seats here I'd like to sit with you."

Bernardo shrugged his shoulders, and she dragged her heavy valise from the passageway into the compartment. Smiling at him, she made a feeble attempt to lift it up to the luggage net above them. Bernardo remained seated and the suitcase stayed on the floor near the door.

There were very few people on that carriage going straight to Paris, and no one else in their compartment. The woman sat across from him next to the window, and kept looking absent-mindedly out into the station until the train departed.

As soon as the train had picked up speed and they were already in French territory, she got up and slowly took off her jacket and hung it. Bernardo watched her. A tight blouse confirmed the bust, waist and derriere on her shapely, lithe body. Not only that: When she crossed her legs, the soft skin of her knees allowed him to imagine her smooth thighs. She was without question a very attractive woman. His rage about what he had gone through evaporated little by little in such agreeable company.

The trip would have continued without note if she had not asked a question out of the blue. "It's beautiful, eh?"

Beautiful? What? Ah! The little inlaid watch hanging from a gold chain and resting at the base of her décolletage between the harmoniously rounded advertisements for her breasts.

"Yes, it's beautiful," he answered, somewhat embarrassed.

"And this, what do you think?" She showed him a handsome ring with a miniature watch.

She proceeded with her entire showcase: Two on her wrist, another on her forearm. And finally, with a light and impish chuckle, though apparently without intent to arouse, she pulled on her skirt and showed him her thigh, which conformed to Bernardo's earlier fantasy of perfection. Around its circumference she had a wide belt well packed with several watches.

"It's beautiful, eh, my friend?" She laughed with a shameless audacity that for the first time distorted that innocent and almost childlike face.

A fascinated Bernardo responded, yes, it was "beautiful," but in truth he was not looking at the watches but at her curvaceous body, her provocative neckline, and above all her thigh. *Damn, is she hot!*

The expression occurred to him and went straight to his conscience. Immediately he grasped his situation. He jumped up brashly without another word, grabbed his suitcase and stormed out of the compartment like a hurricane.

"*Monsieur! Monsieur!*" he heard the woman calling after him.

He did not go back. He distanced himself through the corridors of every car until he arrived at the other end of the train.

"*Votre billet, s'il vous plait...*"

Bernardo showed his ticket and invented some explanation for his change of seat. The conductor put him in another carriage, and Bernardo continued on to Paris.

He lay back and tried to sleep, but it was difficult. Successive pictures came into his brain. The scene at Customs? The suitcase heavy with chocolates? The suspicions they directed against him? The nervousness he felt? His gorgeous valise disemboweled? The showcase of contraband watches and rings?

No. In his obsessive memory, very different images came to him again and again. The innocent smile, the lovely woman's body outlined under that form-fitting blouse, the roundness of those breasts peeking out of her décolletage, and that perfect thigh daringly rising above that knee.

SAS baggage check in at Bromma International Airport BMA, Stockholm, 1950s (SAS Scandinavian Airlines, public domain)

When You Least Expect It

1

THE policeman took his passport, examined it slowly without any apparent reaction and finally, turning toward Flávio, signaled that he exit the line and go back.

Flávio extended his hand so that the policeman would return his passport, but the officer simply repeated his gesture and paid him no further attention.

He went back and waited. What calamity could the police have found in his passport?

The other passengers passed through control, the line finished, and Flávio remained in the large deserted space behind the passenger control gate.

After some minutes, he approached the counter once again. The agent who had attended to him before was no longer there, and his colleague, with no explanation, repeated the gesture the other had made—for Flávio to go back.

This was a complicated situation. They wouldn't allow him to enter Italy and were leaving him like this in the airport, without documentation, without knowing what was going on or knowing what to do.

He waited for a protracted hour roiling with annoyed impatience.

He was getting ready to go to the airline company desk when the first policeman appeared. He motioned him to come to the control counter and, again without saying a word, handed him the passport.

Flávio left the airport and picked up the first train to Rome.

What a strange story.

2

He related to his Italian comrades what had happened.

"Maybe the passport had expired," one of them speculated in Italian. "Or maybe it's not valid for our country."

They'd have to see. An old comrade specializing in these things since the time of Mussolini and the Nazi Occupation, would discover the reason for what happened. They brought Flávio to his house.

Rodolfo Pertini was an aged man, bald, with a drawn face and chrome-framed eyeglasses.

They sat across from one another at a long table with a wooden surface and an overhanging lamp whose shade pointed down.

Pertini would speak Italian, and Flávio in Portuguese. Pertini would understand.

Pertini took the passport and as he slowly leafed through it, made relevant commentary.

So much travel through so many countries, one after another, so many visas in so many languages. There's not a policeman in the world who wouldn't be suspicious.

"They're not my trips," Flávio explained. "Several comrades have used it."

"That's evident."

Who could believe that a single person would do nothing but travel? And if it were one person, what would he be doing?

He thumbed through the document once more.

"It's dangerous using a passport like this," he declared.

"Maybe there wasn't another," Flávio said by way of justification.

"Of course, of course."

They continued talking as Pertini continued his examination. Whoever did this work did a fine job. They should be proud. But a passport just can't be used this much.

Now his inspection proceeded more slowly, with a loupe in his hand, page after page, resting from time to time on a single page, pausing and comparing various pages.

"It's not you they found suspect, it's the passport."

He continued his examination, quiet now and paying close attention. Suddenly he stopped, and in his soft, soothing voice, but with an unexpected tone of triumph, he exclaimed, "Aha! This is it!"

"It" was two stamps in different colors, with the same date and at the same border, erroneously superimposed. The departure from Portugal had been stamped after the entry into Spain.

A lay person would never have seen it, but nothing escaped Rodolfo Pertini.

All those stamps, visas, border crossings, corresponding to the unbelievable travels of one single person, were false. They were created so perfectly and impeccably, however, that it would be difficult to prove it. No question about it, in those two erroneously superimposed stamps lay the evidence of a false passport. Surely, at the Milan passenger control they had detected this flaw, yet still entertained their doubts. But he, Pertini, had no doubt.

Flávio should keep it as long as he was in Italy. In any event, it would be risky to continue his travels with that passport. At another control, things could go from bad to worse. They would have to find another way.

As Flávio got up to leave, Pertini asked him to stay a moment. He rose slowly, left the room and returned with coffee. By his manner, and the way he moved around the house, Flávio assumed he lived alone.

"One or two spoons?" Pertini asked with the sugar bowl in hand.

"Two."

They sipped. "Wonderful coffee!" Flávio said.

"Yes, in Italy we know how to do it," Pertini agreed.

After a brief silence, he abruptly asked, "Have you ever been in prison?"

"No, I haven't."

"It's a good thing you haven't."

Pertini uttered this sentence in his same quiet, low voice, but Flávio sensed in it that this man had been imprisoned himself, and certainly suffered a great deal.

3

A proposed solution emerged in a couple of days. They could drive him to Switzerland by car and from there, with a new passport, he could proceed directly to his destination, Prague.

With Donato, he traveled by train to Milan. People were waiting for them there. Rossana, a vivacious young woman, drove them by car to a restaurant where, at her suggestion, they leisurely enjoyed a *lasagna verde al forno* paired with a wine that the waiter recommended.

"*È veramente eccezionale!*" Donato gushed. "Truly exceptional!"

"Indeed!" Flávio agreed, though thinking to himself that Portuguese wines were much better.

Halfway through the meal, a comrade came to join them. He shortly left with Donato, and didn't return.

"It's all set," Donato reported as he returned to the table. They would go by car to Zurich. There Flávio would receive his ticket and a new passport. The flight to Prague was direct, and the Czech comrades would be waiting for him at the airport.

An uneventful and most agreeable car trip followed. The whole afternoon they drove through the north of Italy, making stops, admiring the scenery, getting out of the car for a look-see around the streets and buildings of small cities, sitting on one or another esplanade drinking coffee. Rossana told her stories, sometimes in Italian, other times in French. Flávio didn't always understand what they were about, but by her smile and the expressions on Donato's face, he figured they involved some kind of mischief.

As night fell, they parked the car on the lovely piazza of a small town, and Rossana led them to a restaurant.

"*Lasagna verde al forno?*" the waiter suggested.

"Ah, no," Rossana interjected. "You'll think we have nothing else to offer you!" And she ordered the *tagliatelle alla bolognese.* Pasta and macaroni were not Flávio's favorites, but he had liked the lasagna and the tagliatelle even better.

It was dark when they got on the road again, Rossana driving hours on end, pensive and careful at the wheel. Now and then they passed through little villages. They saw nothing of the scenery, just, lit up by the headlights, the road and the curb. After the straight roads and gentle hills, they were now climbing steep inclines with sharp curves, the indications of mountainous terrain.

After midnight they stopped in a small settlement and walked into a modest hotel.

They were, of course, expected. After a brief greeting, and without asking for any identity or documents, the employee on duty showed them their rooms.

They departed well before sunrise. Strangely, Rossana drove through narrow, twisting, empty streets of the town before she took once again to the highway.

As day broke, a new landscape appeared—a long, green valley, with snow-covered mountain peaks on the horizon.

"When will we cross the border?" Flávio asked.

"We're in Switzerland, comrade," Rossana laughed.

4

In Zurich they accompanied Flávio to the airport. Rossana handled the check-in just in time. Only when Flávio got in line for the police control did Donato, who had forgotten until now, hand Flávio his new passport. At the control, they stamped it, Flávio put it in his pocket, gave a wave goodbye to the comrades and then had to run to the plane with the other passengers, where he took his assigned seat.

A sense of relief and safety overcame him. Now he could sleep peacefully. In an hour and a half he'd arrive in Prague, where the comrades would be awaiting him at the airport.

He awoke to the violent thump of the landing gear on the tarmac.

The plane skidded crazily down the runway and finally, shuddering with the strong application of the brakes, slowed down until it stopped in front of the terminal.

Flávio was in no rush. Now he had time. He watched the usual excitement as the passengers stood up, put on their jackets, adjusted their clothing, and retrieved their luggage from the baggage racks.

But he jumped with fright when he saw that the police advancing toward him down the aisle were not the Czech police, but French police!

Quite upset, he quickly found a stewardess. "*Il y a une erreur!* There's some mistake! This is not my flight! I was going to Prague, not to France."

"Oh, but this is your plane, *monsieur*." Now, once a week, they made a stop in Paris.

"*Votre passeport, monsieur*," the policeman reached his hand out.

Flávio gave it to him, naturally.

And now? The passengers had to deplane and be ready to depart in an hour. How was he going to get out of this mess? The passport was now in the hands of the police, and he didn't even know what name was on it. He couldn't ask for it back, nor could he respond when they would eventually call for him. *Now I'm in big trouble*, he thought. *We sure screwed that up.*

He left the plane with the others and, upon thought, concluded there was only one solution—to be the last passenger called to reboard, because by that time the police would only have one passport left, his.

After an hour, the passengers gathered to reembark. Control announced the names—Rossi… Amalato…Gilbert…Smith… Vitorini….

He deliberately kept behind, not knowing whether they had called his name or not. He was the last one to approach the police.

"Monsieur Gabarini—"

Was that him or not?

"*Oui.*"

"I already called your name several times—"

"*Excusez-moi*," Flávio said, pointing to his ears as if to say he was hard of hearing.

He went through, seated himself, somewhat rattled, and after almost two hours in the air, wide awake and still experiencing the uncertainties and anxieties of the trip, arrived in Prague.

There were the comrades on the landing strip. They themselves asked for his passport and took care of everything. Leaving the airport, a Tatra took them to the hotel.

They asked how the trip went.

"Everything good," he responded.

Naturally there were lessons to be learned from what happened. But this was neither the place nor the time to study and analyze so many failures.

Pjotr Mahhonin, PVL-109 *Valvas* lifeboat 1, Lennusadam, Tallinn, 2017 (Creative Commons)

The Whaleboat and the Cuddy

1

AT the appointed hour, the car traveled slowly in the semi-darkness on the quay, stopped gently and turned off the head-lights. To its side, bathed in fog, hunkered the black, majestic bulk of the ship, its profile cut by the clear, slanted line of the gangway rising up to its gate.

There was a quick, wordless goodbye: Everything had been said and done as expected. He exited the car, which once again lit up the pier with its headlights until it disappeared into the darkness ahead.

Saul found himself alone on the empty dock. The seaman Joseph was supposed to be waiting for him. Without wast-ing any time, Saul hurriedly crossed the cement platform and stepped up on the gangway. At the top, he stood facing the vast and still barely discernible upper deck. It was an immense, vacant space, without a person or movement or sound. With no sign of life at all, it might have been an abandoned ship. A strong sign of his surroundings came from the humid, salty

aroma of port waters, mixed in with a heavy accent of petro-
leum oil.

He stood motionless next to the gate. Contrary to agreement, Joseph was not waiting for him there. What to do? Give
up and go back? Retreat down the gangway, leave the ship
behind, and then what? He didn't even know how to get out
of the port, much less find his friends.

At the far end of the deck, toward the stern, he made out
the contours of the ship and the profile of the smokestack. If
there was anyone on board, if Joseph were awaiting him, he
could only be there. Without giving it any more thought, Saul
decided to walk in that direction through the wide, dark space.

Only at the very farthest end did he see Joseph, standing
almost hidden in the shadows as though he had nothing to do
with him. Joseph was alert, however. "*Viens!*" he whispered.
"Come!"

Saul followed.

2

Holding him by the arm, Joseph led him on a tortuous course
of curves and narrow metal staircases. They ended in complete
darkness in an airless, closed compartment. Joseph helped him
lie down somehow and covered him with a blanket.

"*Ne bouge pas, je reviens.* Don't move, I'll be back," he said in
a low voice.

Saul waited. The silence and immobility were broken at
last by a massive jolt, followed immediately by the deafening,
powerful din of the ship's engines.

Joseph returned, holding a flashlight. He took off the blanket, had Saul stand up, and then opened the door to a tall,
narrow cuddy. At first Saul did not understand what Joseph
wanted.

"*Vite, vite,*" Joseph urged. "Quick, we only have a few minutes." And without any further explanation, he pushed him
inside the closet, helped him in with a couple of good shoves,
and shut the door. Suddenly Saul felt himself in total darkness, violently squeezed into a space he didn't really fit, stuck,
compressed and boxed in without being able to make any

movement and hardly able to breathe. It was as though he had been shut up in a coffin—with only one difference, and for the worse. He was upright, not horizontal.

He heard footsteps and voices. In front of the cuddy people spoke in muted voices. Then more footsteps, and once again the loud roar of the engines, the rumble of the entire hull, and the rhythmic rocking of the ship on the water.

For hour after interminable hour, Saul had no choice but to remain in his untenable position. He had unbearable pains in his legs, neck, chest and arms. He could hardly breathe. He couldn't take it any more, couldn't resist. Infinite time passed without end. If it continued like this, he'd wind up shouting for someone to let him out of there, whatever the consequences might be.

The cuddy door opened unexpectedly. Now, with the aid of a flashlight, Joseph, accompanied by another seaman, supported him to keep him from falling. Joseph held a glass in his hand and offered it to Saul. "Drink up! It'll do you good!"

Hardly able to keep himself upright, sopping with a cold sweat, Saul took a swig. The comforting alcohol quickly diffused through his body.

The two seamen lost no time. With their flashlight turned off, they led him through the dark up a series of stairways. At the top of the ship they came out into the fresh, damp air. Again, it smelled of oil and gasoline mixed with ocean aromas.

Everything happened fast. They led him to a whaleboat, whose canvas covering had been untied, and helped him to climb in. They tossed two packages inside, skillfully retied the canvas cover, and walked away.

It was complicated getting comfortable. The covering almost brushed the whaleboat benches, and only between benches or under them could he extend his legs. He adjusted himself as well as possible. After what he had endured in the cuddy, this felt like relief. At last he was installed in the place he was promised to reach his country.

The ship was now sailing the open seas. The cool air of early morning entered through the canvas cover's semicircular openings. After so many hours of tension, he felt peaceful and safe.

3

That didn't last long. At the bottom of the boat, a rope ladder with hard knots like stones prevented him from lying down. He tried, but it was impossible. With the rocking of the ship, he found no comfortable position.

On the first day, with a calm sea, a few surprises distracted him. Through the openings in the canvas cover he could see a slice of blue, sunny sky. Cawing seagulls flew in the ship's wake as the vessel continued sailing to the regular, monotonous sound of the whirling propellers.

And so he passed the interminable day, nibbling from time to time on his provisions, drinking gulps of water, and trying in vain to find a position in which he could sleep.

The second day was marked by an unexpected occurrence. Saul heard voices approaching him, joking and laughing, and sounds of great excitement. Then it was quite a shock when vigorously sprayed water entered the whaleboat. Once, twice, three times, with the raised seamen's voices now quite close to him.

It was the day for swabbing the deck. Saul was left drenched and freezing.

4

The storm came on during the night, announcing itself little by little, insistently and inevitably. At first it didn't disturb the rhythmic *whup-whup* of the propellers. Occasional blows from waves breaking on the prow made the whole ship shake with ferocious resonance. Later, ever stronger, came the slaps, the shivers and rocking. The blowing wind went from hushed flurries to moaning to sharp whistling, to giant heaving in the roaring waves and tormented ocean. Overflowing the gunwales, torrents of water swept over the deck from end to end. At certain moments the ship seemed at the mercy of the tempest. With the prow in the trench of the waves and the stern out of the water, the propellers rotated in space with an angry metallic sound that cut through the crashing storm.

It lasted for hours. Then the storm moved on as it had come. The whistling, shouting winds gradually became less aggressive. The powerful impact of the waves against the hull gave way to the more normal rocking of a ship as the seas became less dramatic. From frenetic agitation and hits and slaps, the ship little by little started moving more calmly, in friendly, harmonious cooperation with the ocean surface.

The storm had passed.

5

The third day was a monotonous one on calm seas. Despite being bruised and hurt, and having found no good position, Saul did fall into short spells of deep sleep. He fell asleep once more as evening shadows gathered.

It was still night when he awoke, reacting to something new. Now the engines were murmuring lazily. Rocking gently, the ship had stopped.

Joseph and his comrade appeared and deftly untied the canvas cover. They looked into the whaleboat. "Quick, hand me your waste bucket."

Joseph passed the bucket to his friend who immediately, in one long throw, tossed it overboard.

"Grab your things and come. Quick!"

Saul scrambled between the cover and the boat and jumped out awkwardly. Just as they had done a few days before, the two seamen hastily led him away in the dark.

When they stopped and lit their flashlights, Saul saw himself in front of that cursed cuddy where he thought he would lose his life.

"Oh, no! Not this!" he protested.

They didn't even respond. They pushed him forcefully into the narrow space, made him turn around facing the door, and once again shut him in.

Saul had known hard times in his life, moments at which he felt the nearness of death. But those painful hours spent in the darkness of that closet seemed to him like the most painful ever. Forced to stand at attention, without being able to make any movement, his face hitting the door every time he adjusted his neck, he felt a mad desire to move, to sit, to breathe, to put an end to all this.

Never, ever, ever will it end. I can't bear it any longer, I can't, I can't. No more, no more.

The ship, having started up its engines and set sail again, now stopped, and the sound of the propellers died away. Voices could be heard, and small movements of the ship could be felt, forward, back and to the side. Saul had the impression they were docking.

Then everything spun out in a whirlwind. Joseph opened the cuddy, holding Saul up so that the half-dead man wouldn't collapse and, giving him a swig of brandy, checked that he was steady on his feet.

"Nous y sommes, mon vieux. We have arrived, old man."

Quickly he told him what to do. He should go out and cross the deck. Don't hesitate, and don't look at anyone. Go straight to the gate and down the gangway to the pier. "I'll be right behind you."

6

That was the agreement. Joseph would secure the disembarkation pass of another sailor and the two of them together would pass through the maritime police control and the gate with access to the outside.

Although still a little unsteady on his feet, Saul did as Joseph had said. Leaving the shadows of the corridor for the deck under a beating sun, he was surprised by all the intense, busy motion. Sailors were talking, walking and carrying different things. Saul proceeded through all the hustle and bustle. He was shocked that no one looked at him. He got to the gate and the gangway descending to the dock. He looked back, expecting Joseph to be trailing close behind.

But no, he hadn't come. Something screwed up again. And the worst of it, that it happened now, at the end, at his arrival home. Would Joseph do as he did when Saul boarded the ship? How would he pass through control if he didn't have the disembarkation pass? But there was nothing else he could do. He walked down the gangway, trying to do it neither hurrying nor too slowly, and when he stepped onto the dock it hit him like a lightning bolt that he was finally back in Portugal.

A couple of dozen meters ahead, a maritime police agent in a white cap looked at him intently, seeing him there by himself.

In a sudden inspiration, Saul turned around, looking at the ship's gate, and in the best French pronunciation he could muster, he shouted, "*Eh! Tu viens, quoi?* Are you coming?"

For another few seconds, the policeman with the white cap stood looking at him. But then Joseph appeared and walked down the gangway. Saul waited for him below. He had his back turned to the policeman, who never stopped observing him. The two comrades met up and walked straight to the window at the port exit. Joseph knew the way well.

Always so quiet, now he didn't stop talking, loudly in French, until they got to the control. It was easy, after all. Joseph handed him the other sailor's pass, they showed the passes at the window, and there they were, outside the port. In a hundred meters or so was a semi-deserted street with shops on both sides and old yellow houses. Another street was different, with heavy commerce and crowds of people.

After passing through control, Joseph had quieted down. He started talking again only when they halted at the entrance of a bar. "Have a drink?" he asked.

They went in, drank, and left. After a few steps they stopped again and shook hands cordially.

"Take care of yourself, comrade," Joseph said.

"Perhaps we'll see each other again some day," Saul answered.

The crowds intensified on the street. A steady stream of workers quickened their pace.

From the port, now some distance away, came the muffled sound of a ship's whistle.

It Was Nothing—A Vacation

FERNANDO and Regina agreed to go abroad to take an assignment in a distant country. They felt well prepared for this job of several years' duration.

The stumbling block was Belinha, their four-year-old daughter. They did not want to leave her in the care of her grandmother or their comrades. Without her, they were not inclined to go. But with her, it wouldn't be easy. To reach France, the couple, both underground militants, had to jump two borders, too much of an ordeal to allow the child to accompany them.

They searched out a solution, and the teacher Albino turned up to offer one. He also had a daughter Belinha's age. He and his wife could easily drive Belinha to Paris by car.

They explained to Belinha that during the trip she would not be Belinha but Mimi, the couple's daughter. She appeared to understand the plan perfectly, and the trip took place.

What a wonderful time! They made stops, they slept overnight in two cities, and acted like real tourists—the zoo, a movie, pastries, chocolate and ice cream.

Her parents had endured quite a bit of trouble during their clandestine border crossings, but they said nothing of it to their daughter. Their reunion was quite joyous.

Someone who knew about the lives and travels of the family asked the girl what a clandestine border crossing is like.

Belinha didn't hesitate. "It's nothing—a vacation."

The person who heard that believed it and told it to many others. And many others also believed what the young girl had said.

A short biographical note on the author

Manuel Tiago

MANUEL Tiago was the pen name of Álvaro Cunhal. Edições Avante! in Lisbon, has published nine titles by Manuel Tiago: *Até amanhã, camaradas* (Until Tomorrow, Comrades), which was adapted as a Portuguese television series in 2005; *A estrela de seis pontas* (The Six-Pointed Star); *A casa de Eulália* (Eulalia's House); *Fronteiras* (Border Crossings); *Um risco na areia* (A Line in the Sand); *Os corrécios e outros contos* (The Slackers and Other Stories); *Sala 3 e outros contos* (The 3rd Floor and Other Stories); and *Lutas e vidas* (Struggle and Life). *Cinco dias, cinco noites* (Five Days, Five Nights), adapted to film in 1996, was the first of his works of fiction to appear in English. In its continuing series of Manual Tiago books, International Publishers has so far released *Five Days, Five Nights, The Six-Pointed Star, The 3rd Floor and Other Stories of the Portuguese Resistance*, and now *Border Crossings*.

Álvaro Cunhal was born in Coimbra, Portugal, on November 9, 1913. He began his revolutionary activity as a student at the law school (Faculdade de Direito) of Lisbon. He participated in the student movement and was elected in 1934 as the student representative to the University Senate. He was a militant in the Federation of Portuguese Communist Youth (Federação da Juventude Comunista Portuguesa), and was elected its secretary-general in 1935. In that year he went underground and participated in Moscow in the Sixth International Communist Youth Congress. He joined the Portuguese Communist Party (Partido Comunista Português, PCP) in 1931.

Arrested in 1937 and 1940, and subjected to torture, he returned to political struggle as soon as he was freed after several months in prison. He participated in the reorganization of the PCP in the early 1940s. Again living clandestinely, he was a member of the party Secretariat from 1942 to 1949.

Arrested anew in 1949 and brought before a fascist court, he delivered a ringing denunciation of the fascist dictatorship and a defense of his party's program. Judged guilty, he remained for 11 years in fascist prisons, almost eight of them in complete isolation. On January 3, 1960, he escaped from the prison fortress at Peniche together with a group of brave communist militants. Once again called to the Secretariat of the Central Committee, he was elected Secretary General of the PCP in 1961.

Living abroad, in Moscow and Paris, from that time forward he participated in numerous congresses and gatherings with communist parties and other revolutionary forces in international conferences. He played a critical role in organizing worldwide support, especially within the socialist countries, for the independence movements in the far-flung Portuguese colonies in Africa.

After the downfall of the fascist dictatorship on April 25, 1974, he served as Minister without Portfolio in the first four provisional governments, and was elected as a deputy to the Constituent Assembly in 1975 and to the Assembly for the Republic in 1975, 1979, 1980, 1983, 1985 and 1987. He was a member of the Council of State from 1982 to 1992.

In accordance with the decisions made at the 14th Congress of the PCP in 1992 concerning renewal and a new structure of leadership, he stepped down as Secretary General of the PCP and was elected by the Central Committee as President of the National Council of the party.

In December 1996, the 15th Congress of the PCP eliminated the National Council of the party and its presidency. Cunhal was re-elected as a member of the Central Committee.

He was re-elected to the Central Committee at the 16th and 17th party congresses in December 2000 and November 2004 respectively.

Under his own name Cunhal published several books about politics. He was a gifted artist as well: A book of his collected drawings has appeared. In addition, he published an original translation of Shakespeare's *King Lear*.

He died at the age of 91 on June 13, 2005. His funeral in Lisbon was attended by half a million people. He had one daughter, Ana Cunhal. The Portuguese government issued a postage stamp in his memory and later, in 2021, another stamp commemorating the centennial of the PCP to which he had devoted his life.

About the Translator

ERIC A. Gordon, a Los Angeles resident since 1990, is a native of New Haven, Connecticut. His undergraduate degree is from Yale University, where he majored in Latin American Studies, studying Spanish five years and Portuguese two years. He also took a summer residency in Portuguese at New York University. He went on to Tulane University, where he continued studying Portuguese and wrote a master's thesis on the opera in Rio de Janeiro in the 19th century, using original sources uncovered in the Arquivo Nacional. He earned a doctorate in history, also from Tulane, writing his dissertation about the anarchist movement in Brazil in the pre-World War I era. He also studied Portuguese language and culture under a Gulbenkian Foundation fellowship in Lisbon.

International Publishers initiated its Manuel Tiago series in 2020 with Gordon's translation of *Five Days, Five Nights*, followed by *The Six-Pointed Star, The 3rd Floor and Other Stories of the Portuguese Resistance*, and now *Border Crossings*. When complete, the series will comprise all nine works of fiction by Álvaro Cunhal, each appearing for the first time in English.

Gordon is the author of *Mark the Music: The Life and Work of Marc Blitzstein,* and co-author of *Ballad of an American: The Autobiography of Earl Robinson*. A memoir in short story form that he translated from Portuguese, *Waving to the Train and Other Stories*, by Hadasa Cytrynowicz, appeared in 2013 from Blue Thread Press. In 2015 he executive produced the compact disk *City of the Future: Yiddish Songs from the Former Soviet Union*, a collection of songs composed in 1931 by Samuel Polonski to the lyrics of major Soviet Yiddish poets. He is the author of a currently unpublished political autobiography.

From 1995 to 2010, Gordon was Director of the Workers Circle/ Arbeter Ring in Southern California. He previously worked at Social and Public Art Resource Center, helping to produce murals all around the city of Los Angeles, which gave him the experience to commission a mural at the Workers Circle building. He was Southern California Chapter Chair of the National Writers Union (Local 1981 UAW/AFL-CIO) for two terms. He has written for dozens of local, national, and international publications, mostly about art, music, culture, and politics. From 2014 onward, he has been a staff writer and editor for *People's World* online newspaper.

From 2006–09 Gordon took coursework toward certification as a Secular Jewish Leader, referred to in Yiddish as a *vegvayzer*. Upon graduation, he became a legal officiant certified to conduct weddings and other ceremonial functions, a role equivalent in law to a minister, priest, or rabbi. He has a similar endorsement as a Humanist celebrant for people of any background. For five years he served as a Deputy Commissioner of Civil Marriage for the County of Los Angeles, where he conducted 1500 marriages.

Eric A. Gordon can be contacted at ericarthurgo@gmail.com.

Questions to Ponder and Discuss

ONE of most critical issues in underground work, perhaps in politics and life in general, is risk assessment. Alfredo took considerable risk in volunteering to escort Barra out of Portugal in "Spain Lies to the East." What factors go into a decision that distinguish acceptable risk from adventurism?

Toward the end of the story, after Alfredo returns home and with his girlfriend Sílvia's help has slept off his exhaustion, the author writes, "Smiling and in good spirits, Alfredo pulled her into the sheets. They got up when it was already getting dark." Clearly Tiago is signaling a long desired-for physical reencounter with a "happy ending." Sexual intercourse shows up in other Tiago books as well, and generally also in the same restrained or metaphorical terms. Why is such a worldly man and writer such as Álvaro Cunhal so reticent?

In "The Pass Through the Pyrenees," the first guide insisted that Abel and Francisco discard their shoes and change into canvas espadrilles. This was obviously a long-established protocol for such crossings. Why?

At one point, when the two border jumpers realized they had left their food packet behind, their second guide "had stepped away for a moment," a discreet way, it would seem, of saying he had gone to relieve himself. We hear very little about the ways in which the characters in this book (and in other Manuel Tiago titles as well) take care of their bodily functions. Do you think such modesty on the author's part is warranted? Why is he so reserved about these natural functions? They might have provided some amusing episodes! No doubt, this question is related to his diplomatic treatment of sex.

In this third story of the book, we have already seen the importance for three times in a row of "safe houses," where comrades were hidden, protected and cared for. Later stories also include this feature. It's what Miguel and Sofia will be setting up in the outskirts of Lisbon in the story "An Uncommon Education" in *The 3rd Floor and Other Stories of the Portuguese Resistance*. Under what circumstances, if any, do you think you would be prepared to serve in that capacity, giving refuge to a wanted political figure or an escapee from jail?

"From Gascony to Portugal" is this book's most complex story in terms of length, the variety of its characters, and the fascinating way the author goes back to the horrors of World War II and Franco fascism in Spain to set the scene. Yet he is also quite philosophical when it comes to parsing out the often difficult bonds within a family: "These are the mysteries that no one explains and no one dares be explained. Such respectable enigmas in human relationships gain significance over time for being just what they are, great unknowns that command respect. That is when, in relationships between and among people, all is right and clear with safe and tranquil serenity." What's your response to that? How does it apply to the Dupré family? Does it ring true in families you know, perhaps your own?

In "Women Over the Soajo" we meet two feisty, self-assured women who are confident they can handle any challenge that comes their way. But we also meet their "handlers" who will guide them over the border and are not pleased to find out their comrades are two women. In your experience, is male chauvinism (the term used in that period), or sexism today, still a significant issue in left and progressive movements?

Do you think you could have withstood the torture that Carlos suffered in "The Hold?" Well, at least the comrade shipmates supplied him with a pail for his waste! A common perception that has come down to our day is that Yugoslavia was only a peripheral member of the Soviet Bloc, rather independent in its policies and far more open to the West in terms of tourism and movement in and out of the country of its own citizens. But here we see a side of the story that places Yugoslavia firmly in the constellation of socialist countries that were happy to give aid to resisters against Portuguese fascism. Does this alter your perception in any way?

Speaking of material aid to Portuguese resisters, how about those suitcases that got mixed up—the one with the luxury furs and the other with rather incriminating contents regarding guerrilla warfare? Could a violent régime be overthrown by nonviolent means? (Hint: In Cunhal's report to the Central Committee in 1964, and in the Party program of 1965, the PCP formulated the strategy of a national uprising and the eight points of the national and democratic Revolution, which in broad lines were confirmed in the 25th of April Revolution of 1974.)

"In Brazen Pursuit" could be summed up with that familiar aphorism, "Just because you're paranoid doesn't mean you're not being followed." Tiago recognized there's a place for appreciating the comic and the absurd even in the midst of the most serious of circumstances. Were you surprised by the twist ending? Have you had comparable experiences where the serious and the comic are so inextricably intertwined?

In some ways, "By Train Through Nazi Germany" represents a turning point in the cocky Vito's coming of age. Again, the author mixes fascistic terror with the young man's humorous perceptions. What do you make of Vito's compartment mate, the Englishman P. Brown? Was he telling the truth about what he was doing in the USSR? And what do you make of the two envelopes that, after leaving Soviet territory, he fished out of a secret pocket in his pants and kissed, saying, "Now we are safe?" What do you suppose was in those envelopes?

"Comrade and Gentleman" shows a side of the author we have not seen before—erotic fantasy! Did that surprise you? Was it convincing to you that after all the trouble the woman with the chocolates had caused for him, Bernardo would still be thinking about, uh, her thighs?

Trotsky wrote a book called *Their Morals and Ours*, trying to discern the material and class basis of morals in the world. So is it in the end *moral* to create fake passports, lie about your identity, even to cross borders illegally? What boundaries do we set for the moral guidelines we choose to follow, and who determines them? Are those boundaries applicable to all of society, to just our group, or just to oneself? How much is permissible? What would we refuse to do even if ordered to? Is there a defensible difference between socialist morality and bourgeois morality? Or does that open up the field to a wide array of abuses?

www.ingramcontent.com/pod-product-compliance
Lightning Source LLC
Chambersburg PA
CBHW030533020726
47494CB00004B/1337